SAM CRESCENT

EVERNIGHT PUBLISHING ®

www.evernightpublishing.com

Copyright© 2018

Sam Crescent

Editors: Karyn White

Cover Artist: Sour Cherry Designs

Jacket Design: Jay Aheer

ISBN: 978-1-77339-007-9

SAM CRESCENT

DEDICATION

I would like to say a big thank you to Evernight and to my editor, Karyn White. Without either people The Skulls wouldn't have a home. I have loved this venture into biker romance and I want to say a big thank you to all my readers. You're all wonderful and your words mean so much to me.

SAM CRESCENT

TINY

The Skulls, 4

Sam Crescent

Copyright © 2014

Prologue

Staring at his front door, Tiny knew he'd fucked up bad. He stared at the flowers in his hand knowing they were a pitiful excuse for what he'd done. The moment his wife, Patricia, had walked in his office, he'd felt the guilt slam through him. Even with the guilt he'd gotten angry at her for walking into his club, his domain, and what she'd found had torn through his soul.

To the outside world everyone, even his club, believed his marriage was perfect, and to a point it was. Patricia had given him a daughter, and she settled the anger within him, but he was never satisfied. He loved her with all of his heart, and he'd do everything to make her smile.

Patricia doesn't give you what you need.

Tiny cut the thought away immediately. There was no way he could blame Patricia for what he needed. Not every woman wanted a man to be in charge. It still didn't give him an excuse to do what he did. Patricia gave him more than most women ever had. He'd been using a sweet-butt to rid himself of the stress running The Skulls gave him. Not that fucking everything in sight was an excuse because it wasn't. Since he'd taken out

Snitch and the evil lurking in Fort Wills, Tiny hadn't dealt with anything but tension. He didn't know what happened to Snitch, but as long as the bastard didn't come back, Tiny would be happy. Patricia didn't deserve the way he was treating her, and each time he lost himself in another woman he always promised himself it was going to be the last one.

He heard the loud music from Lash and Nash upstairs. The boys were going to be great when they joined The Skulls. They were good kids considering what they'd lost at a young age. He was already working at patching them in. Opening the front door he walked into his home. The scent of roast chicken greeted him.

"Hello," he said.

No one answered him. From Lash's room rap music was playing. Nash's room had rock music, and his daughter had pop coming from her room. The three different sounds were enough to give him a headache.

Going to the kitchen he found his wife stood at the counter beating something in a bowl. "Have you asked them to turn that shit down?" he asked.

"They're kids. They get to do what they want." Patricia wasn't looking at him. She didn't even give him a glance.

"I got you some flowers."

She finally looked up, and he saw her eyes were red-rimmed. "Are these your guilt flowers?" The spite she felt for him filled her voice. He knew he deserved it and handed her the flowers.

"Take the flowers," he said.

"No." She didn't move other than to continue beating whatever the hell she was beating in her bowl.

"For fuck's sake, Patricia. I'm sorry."

The next move startled him as she threw the bowl she'd been using against the wall. The bowl smashed, and the contents decorated the wall and floor. She turned on him with hands on hips. "No, you're not fucking sorry because it's not the first time. You're never going to fucking change." Her breathing was heavy, and her chest rose and fell with each indrawn breath. The music in the background still played loudly.

Gritting his teeth together, Tiny couldn't stop the arousal at seeing her angry. The fire in her eyes blazed even if they were tear-stained.

"What do you want me to say?" he asked, dropping the flowers to the counter.

"Nothing. I don't want you to say anything."

She swiped the flowers off the counter and walked away. He never liked people walking away from him, especially his wife. Catching her around the waist, he pulled her against him.

"Let me go!" She shouted the words while also trying to head butt him.

"Fuck, stay still, woman. You're not getting away from it, so fucking stop."

After many minutes of fighting Patricia finally calmed down in his arms. "I fucking hate you, and I hate that club." She spun around in his arms cursing at him.

"The club is what keeps you in this lifestyle. We take care of the fucking town. The club is everything."

"And the men are fucking pigs." She spat the words at him. He wasn't hurt by her outburst. Over the last couple of months they'd been arguing more and more. He loved her, but her nagging was really starting to piss him off. No one knew what was going on between them outside of closed doors. They even kept their arguing away from the kids. He didn't know how he did it, only that he did.

"Watch how you speak about my men. They're good men."

SAM CRESCENT

She shook her head. "You don't even see it, do
you? You're an unfaithful bastard. I don't want you
anywhere near me. You had your dick in a whore today,
Tiny." He held onto her arms, but she stopped fighting
him. "You're going to bring Lash and Nash into that
fucking club. What about your daughter, huh? What
about Tate? She's going to end up with one of those
bastards at the club. What are you going to do when you
see one of them treating her like you're treating me?"
With every word she spoke, her voice grew louder.

His anger increased. Tiny released her and faced
his wife. "You knew this when I fucking married you. If
Tate decides to marry one of my men then she's going to
have to buck the fuck up. I'm not holding anyone's
hand."

Patricia slapped him around the face. "She's our
baby." Tiny looked at his wife and raised his hand in the
air. No one slapped him and got away from it.

*Don't do it. You'll cross the line, and you're
better than that.*

She looked at his hand then back at him.

Slowly, he lowered his hand. "If you had a cock
I'd have wiped you out by now."

"Then it's a good job I haven't. Get out, Tiny. I
don't want you near me right now. Tate would be better
off without you for a father," Patricia said.

Tiny watched her walk toward the wall where the
mess was. He wouldn't have hit her, but for a split
second he'd been tempted. No woman hit him, not one.
He was the fucking boss, and even his wife knew the
score. Tiny never hurt women, but he made sure they
answered for their crimes.

You cheated on her, dick.

"Mommy." Tate's voice came from the doorway.
He turned to see his little girl pale. Tate was the light of

his life. Everything he did was to build her a better life. He doubted she'd have anything to do with the club when she was older. If she did, he knew deep down she would keep the man to claim her on his toes.

"Hey, baby."

From the look on her face, he knew she'd heard their argument. Not good. He didn't want anyone to know there was the occasional argument between him and Patricia.

"Not now, Tate," Patricia said.

"I'll deal with her." Tiny left the kitchen going toward his daughter. "How's my little girl?" he asked.

"Are you going to break up? I heard Edward and Nigel say you were." She was the only girl who got away with calling the two brothers by their own names.

"Nah, we're not going to break up. We're just arguing like adults do. I love your mommy so much. I wouldn't let her leave us."

"When I'm grown up I'm not going to argue with my husband."

"You're not?" he asked, heading upstairs.

"No, I'm going to find a boy that will do as he's told, and I can tell him what to do, and I'll never be hurt."

Tiny chuckled. Tate was his whole world. He loved his wife, but at times Patricia was a little temperamental.

The guilt disappeared within a few hours, and that night he made love to his wife. Patricia always responded to him, and it only took a few caresses for her to relent to him.

****

Three years later he was burying her in the ground, and Tiny felt the full effect of what he'd done to Patricia. He was left with three kids and not a clue what to do.

Rubbing his temple, Tiny looked down at the list of babysitters he'd been given by the club. They'd all banded together to help him out after his wife's funeral. Fuck, Patricia was dead, and he couldn't even begin to think about that shit right now.

"Daddy, someone is at the door," Tate said, shouting down stairs.

"Then fucking answer it. It's probably for you." He lifted the phone and started to call around. Lash and Nash didn't need looking after, but he wasn't allowing his daughter alone. He didn't give a fuck what age Tate was. She would have someone home at all times, and he wasn't going to let up on his ideals.

Thirty minutes passed, and Tiny slammed the phone down. When the violence didn't work, he threw the phone across the room, happy when he saw the device shatter. None of the babysitters wanted to work with him, fucking bitches. The sound of feminine giggling pulled him out of his thoughts. Leaving his office he walked toward the sound.

He found Tate sat at the counter watching a woman he'd never seen before cooking at the stove. Tiny paused, staring at her.

"Daddy's going to love you," Tate said, smiling.

"I'm hoping he'll hire me. I like you, Tate." The woman reached over, touching his daughter's hand.

Leaning against the door frame he checked out the woman whom his daughter was bonding to. The woman was fuller than his wife and any woman he'd been with. Her curves were full, but they didn't make him think of her as fat. She was womanly, beautiful actually. Her smile brightened her face, and he even felt a tightening in his groin. Her eyes were a delicate hazel, startling yet firm. Tiny didn't understand what was going on inside him. Simply looking at her was turning him on. He wanted to get to know her name so he could bend her over when they were in private and fuck her.

"Tate, who is this?" he asked.

He wore his leather cut with The Skulls emblem on the back. Pulling the jacket off, he displayed his ink and muscles. His gaze was on the woman, but the woman was smiling at Tate, not paying attention to him. Feeling like an ass, he sat beside his daughter.

"This is Evangeline Walker, Eva for short, Dad. She's here for the nanny position," Tate said.

"Hi, sir, I'm new in Fort Wills, and I'm a hard worker." Evangeline offered her hand. Staring at her pale fingers Tiny scented her fragrance, strawberry. He loved strawberries. Taking the offered hand, he held on tightly.

Eva didn't give him any flirtatious looks. She simply shook his hand and pulled away. He watched her, waiting for her to do something to show her true colors. She went to her bag and pulled out a piece of paper. "Here are my documents."

Checking over her details he saw she was only a few years older than his daughter. She was over eighteen, which he was fucking thankful for, but he didn't like how much younger than him she was. He shouldn't be lusting after a woman so young. From the look of her she was a little too innocent for his taste as well.

"I've not been in a nanny position before, but I would really love to take care of Tate," Eva said.

"Please, Dad, I like her."

Looking down at the paperwork in his hands, feeling his cock stiffen, Tiny knew he didn't have much choice. Tate had lost her mother. He wasn't willing to hurt her anymore. In the last few months Tate had been acting out. Even Nash and Lash didn't like hanging out with her. Seeing her with Eva and the smile twisted something inside him. There was no way he could deny his little girl.

"Sure," he said, staring at Eva. The other woman was finally looking back at him. He felt like he was drowning in her. There was a glint in her eye that made him question her innocent persona.

"I can start right now," Eva said.

"Where are you staying?" Tate asked, after a huge squeal of excitement.

"I'm in a hotel right now just outside of town. I'll find somewhere suitable—"

"You can stay here. Right, Dad. We've got plenty of room," Tate said.

Eva's gaze darted to him, shaking her head. "No, I couldn't impose."

"You're not imposing. You'll be here when I need you. Dad's not always around, and you can spend time with me." Tate was like a dog with a fucking bone. She wouldn't stop talking.

"I really couldn't."

His daughter turned her gaze on him.

"Please, Dad, please, please, please." The begging went on and on.

"You will stay here," he said, keeping his attention on the woman before him.

"Only if you're sure. I really don't want to impose." Eva's hands were held up. He noticed a gold charm bracelet on her wrist. He frowned. There was something about it that struck a chord with him. He didn't know what it was.

"You're not imposing, and I've got shit to do. We'll go and get your crap from the hotel. I've got stuff to do, and I'll set up your earnings and shit." He kept her documents and moved back toward his office.

Tiny heard his daughter squealing and Eva's

nervous giggle. Slamming the doors closed, he cupped his cock. He was rock hard and in need of some relief.

Pulling away, he refused to give in to the call of the woman looking after his daughter. Thinking about everything else, slowly his cock started to deflate. Nothing was ever going to happen between him and Eva. The other woman was way too young, and he wasn't going to let another woman close.

Did you even let Patricia close?

He didn't want to think about it and started working. Eva was just a woman like all the rest. There was nothing important about her.

SAM CRESCENT

Chapter One

One month from Nash

"Give me a heads-up," Tiny said, looking at the
room full of his men. They all looked wound up tight,
and he knew it was hard for them. Nash was sat beside
his brother, and the last time he'd pissed in a cup for
them, the man had been clean. Seeing all of his men
together, free of the past, filled Tiny with pride at what
he'd been able to create in the last twenty years. He, with
the help of his men, had made Fort Wills what it was
today.

"My baby shouldn't be covering the fucking club
in pink shit. Fucking bad for our reputation," Tiny said,
slamming his fist on the table.

"They're having a baby shower. It's quite mellow
considering Tate's in charge," Lash said, chuckling. The
rest of the crew followed suit. "Three of our women are
pregnant. It's the least we can do with all the shit they've
gone through."

The last comment sobered up the whole group.
Tiny didn't break eye contact with any of his men. In the
last few months they'd lost a lot as a group, but Tiny
wasn't going to let anything more happen. The Skulls
and Fort Wills were his home. They were all his family.

"What's happening with Eva?" Nash asked.

"She's staying for the shower, and then she's
gone," Tiny said, running a hand down his face. In the
last couple of weeks he'd not been able to talk her round
to staying with him. What could he really do? During her
time with him Eva had been his everything, yet she was
leaving at the first opportunity. He'd never begged a
woman to stay with him, and he wasn't about to start
even though he wanted to. Eva was in his blood, driving

him to be a better person. Her leaving would hurt deep. She'd stuck around after he fucked other women, the attacks, and even when he'd treated her like shit. Thinking about Eva made him ache to be the better man. He was pissed about her leaving him, but at the same time he understood why she was leaving.

"What about her father? Will he be coming back here? Will Daddy be coming to kick your ass?" Lash asked.

Eva was not just the ordinary woman he'd first thought. She was the daughter of Ned Walker, a legendary fighter who owned a Las Vegas underground fighting ring. The boys thought it was funny his woman was the daughter of one of the toughest men around. Tiny had been shocked about it when he found out the news.

"I don't know. She's not spoken to me in some time." In the last few weeks he'd been trying to figure out who would set some two-bit crooks onto his men. Something wasn't adding up to him, and he didn't know what it was.

Silence fell on the room. He heard the giggles and the girlish music coming from the other room. Tate really loved the attention being lavished on her. Angel and Sophia were in the same boat with his daughter. All three women were pregnant, expecting the next wave of Skull males. He didn't know if he was happy. Every time he looked at Murphy he wanted to slap him on the back and beat the shit out of him for touching his daughter. The emotions were swamping him once again. His baby was pregnant, and there wasn't a damn thing he could do about it.

"The next shipment is scheduled for the eighth," Alex said. "Ned wants this moving no later than that."

The drugs again. Glancing at Nash he saw the

other man was fine. "Do you think you can handle a shipment?" Tiny asked. After the downfall last time, Tiny didn't know if he was ready to have the other man on a drug run.

"I'm good. We need the shit moving. I'm back to business. I fucked up, and I know that. I'm ready to prove myself. I've got your back."

"Good. Who wants to bow out of this run?" Tiny asked. He never forced any of his men to make a run with the drugs if they didn't want to. They all pitched in on other jobs. The drug runs were more dangerous than anything else.

No one put their hands up, not even Killer, which surprised him. The other man had been staying behind to date the other woman he'd seen hanging out with his daughter. With the shit happening in the last few months he didn't know everything that was going on with his men. Tiny knew it was something he needed to change very soon.

"Killer?" Tiny asked, singling him out.

"Got nothing to stay behind for. I'll be joining you and the rest of the crew." Killer didn't flinch or back down.

"Fair enough. We leave on the seventh in the hope of getting the shit moved." He slammed his hand down on the desk signaling the end of the conversation. The men got up leaving the room. The moment the door opened, Tiny got his first real glimpse of the pink. Even the air smelled like strawberries, vanilla, and honey. If his enemies were to see the club they'd be sure to be pissing themselves laughing at his club.

"Do you think doing the shipment is wise? I can tell Ned to hold everything off," Alex said.

"No, we can't wait." Tiny stood then turned away to look out of the window. Something felt way off about everything that was happening. He couldn't put his finger to it, only had a feeling deep in his gut telling him to watch his back. Tiny hadn't felt this way in a long time. He couldn't quite put his finger on the feeling, but he recognized it.

"Think, Tiny. We've got a lot of enemies right about now. I know what you're thinking about Nash and everything." Alex stood beside him.

"What are you thinking?" Tiny asked, curious to know.

"The past can't always stay buried. The past has a way of finding us."

He didn't say anything to Alex's words. His past was not shiny or even great, but it needed to stay in the fucking past. Tiny had done shit in his life he wasn't proud of. The shit he'd done before forming The Skulls would have his daughter and Eva running in the opposite direction. "Do you know anything?"

"No, nothing has been found out, but you and I both know those two-bit crooks didn't set for Fort Wills on their own. This town is bad news to our enemies. Someone was telling them what to do. Someone who knows us and how to get past us."

Tiny agreed. "Whoever is after us has been around home. They've seen us and watched us without any of us knowing it."

"We need to tell the others."

"Not yet. We will when the time is right."

"It's your decision, Tiny. Know I'll be here when you do." Alex moved away from him. "Eva will leave if you don't do something about it."

He froze, turning to look at the other man. "Why are you saying this shit to me?"

"Patricia is dead. She died a long time ago. It's time you moved on."

"She was your sister."

"And she's my *dead* sister. I miss her, but it's time to move on. Waiting around is never good news for a man. Fucking any woman with a warm hole is not going to satisfy you for long either." Alex left the room after his words.

What Alex didn't know was Tiny hadn't missed Patricia in a long time. Yes, he'd taken plenty of mourning, and he'd gone through a stage of hating himself and guilt. The ring he'd once worn was lying in a drawer at his home. Eva had been the one woman plaguing his thoughts for so long. She was living, breathing, and didn't give him shit for being part of the club. Her attitude was always directed at him. There was nothing else he could do about Eva. The sound of the door opening followed by the feminine scent of strawberry swamped him. Evangeline Walker was a mixture of sweetness and tough bitch. In the last few months he'd seen more of the tough bitch than he had in the entire time he'd know her. It was like her father visited Fort Wills and reminded her of who she was. He loved both parts of her, and that was what scared him.

"Are you hiding out in here?" Eva asked. Her voice went straight to his dick, and he was rock hard. The one time they'd been together he'd fucked it up. Tiny remembered every detail of their time together even down to collapsing afterwards beside her. It was not and never would be one of his finest moments. He hated every second of the memory. Tiny had treated sweet-butts better than he had Eva. The one chance he got with her and he'd blown it. He'd gotten her naked, thrust away, found climax in her sweet, tight cunt and fallen asleep afterwards. The memory alone made him feel fucking old.

"I'm not hiding from anyone." Closing his eyes,

he took several deep breaths before giving Eva his attention. She wore a blue dress with a belt around her waist. The fabric pulled in at the waist and flared out at her hips. He didn't know a dress could be so damn seductive and revealing while also covering up her flesh at the same time. Her tits were more than handfuls for him. Tiny recalled her large nipples, which budded when she was aroused. Fuck, his cock pressed against his jeans demanding attention.

Her hair fell around her in waves in some kind of style. She looked sophisticated, beautiful, and everything he couldn't have. Since finding out about her father, he found himself paying more attention to her. Eva was far out of his league even if her father ran an underground fighting ring.

"Could have fooled me. Tate is buzzing with excitement out there. She needs her father. You're going to be a granddaddy before long," she said. Her hands were pressed together in front of her. He wondered what she would do if he pulled her into his arms and kissed her, messing up her outfit.

"Don't talk about me being a granddaddy." Tiny shook his head hating the knowledge that he was getting old.

"You're going to be fifty years old in a few months, Tiny. You better get used to it. There will be a little baby calling you granddaddy, and you'll love it." Eva smiled, taking a step closer to him.

"Are you going to be staying for that?" he asked.

"For what?"

"My birthday?" He didn't give a fuck about his birthday. In the last few years Eva and Tate had celebrated the event with a cake, but he really didn't care for it. Getting old was not fun at all. Every year he was reminded of how long he'd been fighting. What he was fighting, he didn't know anymore. Fort Wills was safe. The past threat hadn't risen up in the last twenty years. Tiny doubted anyone was going to come back now. Twenty years was a long fucking time to hold a grudge.

"I don't know. My dad's coming to pick me up at the end of the week. I'll be out of your hair in no time. You're probably ready to get rid of me." She smiled at him. Her smile didn't reach her eyes.

"You're the one leaving. I've not showed you the door," he said, hating the fact he couldn't beg and wouldn't beg for her to stay.

****

Eva stared at him feeling the intensity of his gaze. Not once had he asked her to stay, and yet she knew it was what he wanted. They were not good for each other. The last few years had confirmed that for her. This game they played was only hurting the both of them. One of them needed to make it stop, and she was going to be the one to do it by leaving. Vegas was her safety ground. Her father would guarantee it.

"Tiny, I've got to go."

If she didn't get out of Fort Wills now then she never would. Eva knew in her heart she would let Tiny walk all over her simply to be near him. Her love of Tate was nothing compared to the feelings this man evoked within her. At times she thought she'd drown on her love for him. No man, not even Gavin, had made her feel this way.

"No, you don't." He took a step closer, and now she had no choice but to back away. His presence alone made her feel like jelly. She took a step back, but Tiny kept on coming. Eva finally stopped with her back against the wall. His hands rested on either side of her head. Tiny was taller than she was, even in her heels. The top of her head reached his chest, and she had no choice but to look up at him. His dark brown eyes, so like Tate's at times, stared down at her. Where Tate's eyes were filled with innocence Tiny's eyes were filled with pain and power. This man knew what he was doing at all times. He had a past, and it was colorful in a bad way.

"What are you doing?" She wasn't afraid of Tiny. He'd done everything he could to protect her over the last few months. She'd been shot and hurt because of his club. No, Tiny wouldn't hurt her, but his enemies would.

"Nothing you don't want." He leaned in close. His breath fanned across her face. She smelled the mints he kept inside his drawer.

Eva kept quiet waiting for his next move. His lips brushed across hers, and she jerked back. She stopped herself from slamming her head against the wall. The small touch was like a bolt of lightning through her body. Her cunt clenched as her nipples hardened becoming attuned to this man before her. He owned her responses. There was nothing else for her to do other than let go.

The door to the room was closed, so no one would interrupt them. No one would dare interrupt them if they saw her enter.

"Open for me," he said.

She opened her lips, and Tiny took the full opportunity, pressing his lips to hers. One of his hands fell behind her head cupping her. His kiss became firmer, more determined to get what he wanted. Eva had never been kissed like this. Their time in Vegas would never prepare anyone for this kind of possession.

His tongue pressed to her lips, and she met him stroke for stroke. She could no longer keep her hands at her side. Running her fingers up his chest she circled the back of his neck, holding on. They moaned, smashing their lips together. The passion took over giving way to the never ending lust crashing through them. His cock pressed to her stomach making his arousal known.

Her panties were soaked from the kiss he was giving her. There was nothing else for her to do other than give him everything. She felt his touch going under her dress pushing the fabric out of the way. Eva didn't want to stop him. The heat threatened to burn her alive.

When he picked her up she squealed shocked by how easily he moved her. In one smooth movement he placed her on the edge of his desk. He was fast, and he pushed her dress up to her waist before settling her back down again. The hard wood desk was cold underneath her ass. She gasped but couldn't think as in the next second his palm was pressed between her thighs.

"This doesn't change anything," she said, moaning.

"Shut the fuck up." He cut off her reply with his lips.

Crying out, she flung her head back exposing her neck. Tiny bit down hard sucking on the flesh. She whimpered as an answering pulse went between her legs. He tore at her panties pulling them from her body.

"Later, tomorrow, in a fucking month, I don't care. We'll deal with it then." His fingers slid between her slit. He touched her clit, circling the nub before going down to her core. "I've got to have you. I need to wipe that fucking memory from your mind."

She knew what he meant. Their time together had been a disaster. Alcohol, anger, and lust didn't make a good combination for either of them.

"Open your legs wider," he said, ordering her around. With the dress around her waist she was free to do as he asked.

He sat down in his chair staring down at her exposed flesh. She was not into waxes or any fancy work down there. Eva trimmed her pubic hair.

"So fucking pretty," he said, staring at her.

Tiny didn't appear to be making a move. He sat in his chair staring at her.

Licking her lips she felt the heat pool within her. He must see the evidence of her arousal. She was struggling to contain her begging.

Within moments, he reached out stroking a finger up her thigh. He stood abruptly, and his hands were at the zipper behind her. Tiny took control removing the dress from her body followed by her bra. She couldn't believe she was stood in his office at the club naked.

He left her side to lock the door keeping the rest of the world out of sight. On his walk back to her she saw the evidence of his arousal pressing against his jeans. She folded her arms across her stomach becoming aware of how many other women he'd brought to this very room to fuck.

Most of the women he'd taken had been slender and younger than she was. The women hanging around the club knew what the score was whereas she wasn't one of them. She would never be a man's casual screw.

"Don't think about them," he said. "There's no one here but you and me, Eva." He cupped her cheek, tilting her head back. The blinds were still open with the sunlight shining through.

When she opened her lips ready to dispute him, Tiny shocked her by pulling his shirt over his head. For a man approaching his fiftieth birthday he sure didn't look like it. He wasn't a spring chicken, but he'd aged well. The wrinkles at his eyes portrayed a wealth of knowledge to her. His muscles were thick from the hours he spent working out. She used to watch him work out amazed at his stamina. In many ways he reminded her of home. Before moving to Fort Wills she helped at the gym her father owned to train his fighters. She watched men work out on a daily basis. Eva knew Tiny would be shocked by how much she'd seen in her life. She had never been naive or innocent. Growing up around fighters took care of that. For the first few years of living here she had been able to feel innocent. The bikers were not as bad as the fighters she'd known. However, Tiny angered her so much she found it hard to keep that part hidden. With the alcohol flowing not long ago, she'd shown another part of herself, and from the way Tiny had been with her, he liked it.

Ink coated his skin. She saw the names of Lash, Nash, Tate, and Patricia. Eva didn't feel jealous of the names. They were all part of him. From the first moment they met there had been chemistry between them. She didn't trust chemistry as she'd felt it once before and been burnt by it.

The symbol of a skull was on his arm leading down to a snake. On another arm clouds and darkness coated his skin with his loved ones shining through. It was like their names were a light in the darkness. Every bit of ink told a tale, and she didn't know every single story, only that each tattoo was part of him.

"I can't change my past," he said.

"I don't expect you to." She placed her palm on his chest feeling the heavy beat of his heart. When she could stand it no longer she moved her hand down to rest at the button of his jeans. "Just like you can't change my past, Tiny. We all have them."

"You've got a past?" he asked, smirking. "I find that hard to believe. You're too innocent for it, baby."

"You'd be surprised. You forget I grew up in Vegas with a fighter. I've got a past." She flicked his button open before sliding his zipper down. "I'm not what you think I am."

"And what do I think you are?"

Smiling, she went to her knees staring up at him from the floor. "You think I'm innocent. You think I need to be protected when the truth is, I don't need anything, Tiny." She pulled his jeans down to his ankles. He still wore boots stopping her progress. Eva didn't care. She could do what she wanted with where his jeans stopped.

"You need to be protected."

"No, I don't." She gripped his cock in her fist and stroked the tip with her thumb. "There's a lot you don't know about me or refuse to know, Tiny."

"You're not made for this life."

"I grew up in a far harsher life." Eva didn't want to delve into her past. Leaning forward she licked the tip of his cock, which she'd been stroking seconds before. His salty pre-cum coated her tongue, and she swallowed him down. There was nothing to stop her. He let out a curse, but instead of pushing her away, his fingers sank into her hair. She'd never been good at keeping her hair bound to her head and loved keeping the length around her in wavy locks. Eva didn't know what it was, but she loved the thought of him pulling on the length, hard and rough. Everything about Tiny was rough with many hard edges making him the man he was. She also saw he had a past that he tried to hide from.

No matter what he did, she knew deep in her heart she would never be afraid of him. Over the years they'd known each other he'd cursed, thrown things, and in all that time he'd never once raised his hand in order to hurt her. In her mind, Tiny was one of the good guys. Being raised alongside a load of underground fighters she'd seen her fair share of domestic problems. Fortunately, her father didn't agree with violence against women, and the men rarely hurt a woman in front of her father while she was there. However, there were a few times she's witnessed the violence a man could inflict on a woman.

Tiny fisted her hair and pulled harshly. She released his cock only to stare up at him. "What the fuck are you doing to me?" he asked. His voice was gruff, and she could tell he was only just keeping his shit together.

"I'm sucking your cock. Don't you want me to?"

"Where is this going to go? You're going to leave at the end of the week." He wouldn't release her hair even as she tried to pull away from him. Tiny kept his grip firm, unrelenting in his possession.

"I'm not sticking around. This is not good between us. It has never been good, not even in Vegas when we left this town behind." Something changed in his eyes. She saw the multitude of emotions wash over him, and they seemed to vanish all at once. Nothing held him in place. Biting her lip, she fisted his length feeling him harden once again. They were not going to get another moment like this.

He really was a magnificent specimen, and she didn't want to miss a moment with him. The length had to be at least eight inches, if not more, and he was thick. No matter how many times she tried to get past their one time together, Eva wouldn't forget how bad it had been. He hadn't lasted longer than fifteen minutes, and most of them were spent pinning her to the bed because he had to fight her.

The memory between them wasn't great, but no matter how hard she tried, Eva couldn't forget about it. The entire night was engrained in her thoughts. Even if their time now went any better she was still leaving. Her time in Fort Wills had come to an end. The pain he'd caused was too much for her to stick around and wait for him. Too many women had passed, and she refused to put up with it. No, she wouldn't be staying, but the only thing she wanted to take back to Vegas with her was one memory of perfection between them. Surely, it wasn't too much to ask?

Chapter Two

Tiny knew what she was thinking about, and he hated it. He hated every single memory of their time together in Vegas. For the first time in his life he'd been embarrassed by the way he'd fucked a woman. He was Tiny, the leader of the Skulls. He alone was the judge, jury, and executioner in his little town, and he hadn't brought Eva to orgasm, not once. His reputation for being a hard man was firm within the community, and he'd built a good reputation for people not to fuck with him, even if they had been doing that the last couple of months. Not only that, he'd also earned himself a reputation with the ladies. Tiny fucked women, and none of them left his cock unsatisfied.

Ever since he lost his virginity at sixteen he learned the fine art of satisfying a woman. Over the years he'd improved his technique and also learned what he liked more. Getting a woman under him was the best kind of release he loved. Having a woman submit to his hard fucking was what he loved. Patricia hadn't liked his brand of fucking. She found him too hard. No matter who he fucked, he was the one in control, never the woman. He set the pace, and he told them what they were going to do.

Fingering the length of her hair, Tiny knew his woman was going to leave. By the end of the week Eva would no longer be part of his life. He'd miss her, but he wasn't the kind of man to beg a woman for anything. Everything about him was focused on control.

Fuck her brains out.

"Vegas was a fucking mistake. I'm not going to let that happen again." He stroked along her cheek, caressing her jaw and going over her lips. Her body was to die for. He couldn't see every curve in the way she was knelt. Tiny was determined to make sure by the end of the day he knew every single part of her, and he wanted to commit it all to memory.

He went back to her hair, stroking the length once again. "If you're not sticking around then I guess we better make the most of this moment." He tightened his fist in her hair. "Suck my dick."

She opened her lips without him having to ask again. He aligned his cock and plundered her mouth. Eva closed her lips around his shaft, sucking him in. Tiny couldn't tear his gaze away. He didn't want to look away as watching her was part of the fun.

With the grip he held on her hair, he pumped his hips sliding deeper into her mouth until he hit the back of her throat. She didn't try to pull away or stop him from thrusting deeper.

Her eyes were on him drawing him in closer. There was something hypnotic about her hazel depths. From the first moment he laid eyes on her, he'd known there was something about her that was special. The way she made him feel terrified him at times. She possessed every part of him, and she didn't even know it.

Pulling out of her mouth he watched her take a breath. He painted her lips with his pre-cum before sliding back in. Over and over he repeated the same motion each time getting closer to orgasm at how she submitted to him.

He wasn't into whips or anything hardcore the media seemed to be having a frenzy over. No one would ever catch him wearing fucking leather pants or demanding people call him Sir and Master. Fuck that. He would always be Tiny. The only element of domination he took seriously was the cuffs and tying a woman down. He loved having his woman open to him so he could do whatever the hell he liked to her.

Patricia never allowed it.

The thought struck him hard. Closing his eyes, he tried to push the memory of his late wife from his mind. His relationship with her hadn't been everything he wanted it to be. In their years together she never once allowed him to tie her down or to be in control. She'd been too afraid and frightened of the real man he was. For some reason she'd built up this imaginary persona of who he was in her mind. The first time he'd held her down and fucked her hard, she'd screamed at him. He remembered the fear and couldn't bring himself to try again. At least their problems had never gotten out to the club. No one knew they were not matched together, but he still loved her.

After that incident he'd taken his pleasure in the sweet-butts who stayed around the compound and who were willing to take what he had to offer, sex—hard, rough, and where he was the one in charge.

Slamming into Eva's mouth he opened his eyes once more to see her taking more of him. He needed to feel if she was wet enough. Did she really want this? There was so much he didn't know about her, and he refused to risk what little they had for sex.

Releasing her, he picked her up and dropped her onto his desk. The computer tumbled to the floor along with some of his pens and pencils. He didn't give a fuck about them.

"What's the matter?" she asked, cupping his face. He didn't answer her and slid a finger between her slick folds.

She was dripping wet, soaking his fingers with her cream.

He stared into her eyes seeing them dilated, and he felt her need. She had to be aching.

"Nothing." He pressed a finger into her cunt. Eva

moaned and moved to the edge of the bed taking more of him.

"I need you," she said. "Fuck me, Tiny. Please."

Her begging was all he needed. Removing his fingers, he licked each digit swallowing down her arousal. She whimpered but made no move to walk away.

"Is everything okay in there, boss?" Zero asked, knocking on the door.

"Fuck off!" Tiny yelled the words. There was no way he was letting anyone interrupt his moment. Eva would leave, and he wouldn't have the chance to rid her of their one and only memory together. There was no way he was letting a woman escape thinking he was bad in bed. No way in hell was he letting that happen. Especially not Ned Walker's daughter either.

"We heard shit breaking," Lash said.

Did he hear a snicker from one of his men?

"The next person to ask me a stupid fucking question will get their dick blown off. Fuck off!" Gripping her hip with one hand, he rubbed his cock through her wet lips. She cried out, and together they both looked down. This was it, their moment together that would change everything.

He was sure the moment he claimed her, Eva wouldn't leave him. She was too fucking loyal to leave him when he'd taken her as his woman. There was no way he'd be apologizing for who he was, and Eva would have to accept him. After everything he'd done, she was still with him.

"Your men are worried about you," she said.

"They can worry all they want." He pushed the tip of his cock into her pussy. Tiny heard her gasp. Looking up he saw she was still watching them together. Tilting her head back with a finger under her chin, he stopped her from looking at where they were joined.

"Look at me," he said, ordering her.

She didn't pull away or try to look elsewhere. He had her attention, and there was no way he was going to lose it.

Moving both of his hands to her hips he took charge and slid another inch inside her. Eva's eyes widened, and she stared at him, biting her lip.

"Let it out, baby. Scream for me," he said.

"They'll know what's going on."

He shook his head. "They won't say fuck all to you. I'll kill any person who makes you feel bad."

The grip he had on her hips helped him to move her to the edge of the desk. In one quick thrust he plundered inside her to the hilt, hitting her cervix. He was a large man and knew some women hurt to take him.

Eva cried out. The sounds she made echoed off the walls, and he loved every single note of her voice. He felt her pulse around him, and he stopped to bask in the feel of her cunt tightening around his length.

He left her hips to cup her face. Her eyes were closed, and she opened them to look at him. "This is how it should have been in the beginning," he said.

Stroking a thumb across her bottom lip, he slammed his lips down on hers. She opened to him, and he pushed his tongue into her mouth.

Her legs wrapped around his waist as he ravished her mouth, taking everything she had to offer and wanting more. He felt her tits pressed against his chest. The hard buds of her nipples poked him as well.

"So fucking sweet," he said, muttering the words against her lips. "We're not leaving this office today. You're mine."

"We're leaving this office, but we can take it back to your home. This is just a taster of what's to come." She wrapped her arms around his neck, taking his lips this time. Neither had moved. His cock was seated deep into her pussy, but he wasn't in a rush to fuck and finish. He would be taking his time, and only when both of them were begging for release would he take them over the edge.

"I can live with that." He moved down to stroke her neck then down farther still to take each of her breasts into his palm. Tiny fingered the hard buds feeling the answering ripple in her cunt. Leaning down he took one between his lips and sucked hard, biting down into her flesh. He wasn't hard enough to draw blood, but he was hard enough to make her squirm on his desk.

Every time he sat at this desk he would remember everything about her. He would remember the way she smelled, her taste, and how she looked when he fucked her.

"Lean back," he said, pulling away until they were only connected by his dick inside her.

She leaned back on his desk, pushing more of his crap onto the floor. It was the best place for all of his shit. He'd pick them up later or get one of his men to put the desk to rights.

Staring down he saw the base of his cock, and her pussy lips were opened around his shaft. Her clit was peeking out, begging him to touch it.

Licking his thumb, he pressed it to her clit. He didn't move but watched her response.

Her arousal flooded his shaft.

"You're mine, Eva. You'll always be mine, and you were mine from the first moment you walked into my house and my fucking life." He gently stroked her clit. His actions showed he wasn't in a rush to end their moment together.

"Stop torturing me," she said, breathlessly.

He wasn't done with what he had planned. "This is my show, baby. You'll get what I'm going to fucking give you."

Slowly, he caressed her clit, feeling every ripple and pulse around his dick. Her cunt was wet and snug. He wasn't ready to leave her or for this to end. No one needed him outside this room.

For a few minutes he could have what he'd wanted for a long time, Eva underneath him, submitting to him.

Being buried inside her helped him to forget everything he'd done to her in the years they'd known each other. Yes, he'd hurt her and been horrid to her. Everything fell away as he stroked her clit, feeling her tighten around him.

****

Tiny was going to torture her until nothing remained of her. Eva was sure of it as he slowly, ever so slowly, caressed her clit. This was nothing like their time in Vegas. This was no rushed fucking or quick release. Tiny was taking his time making her feel everything he wanted her to feel.

Growing in frustration, she glared at him. "You're not being fair."

One of his hands slapped her thigh. The tap burned, but it wasn't painful.

"Does my baby need to come?" he asked, teasing her.

"You know I do. Stop teasing me."

"I've had Vegas hanging over my head, baby. You told all the boys how bad I was. It was the first time I saw the real fire burning within you. This is my chance to prove to you Vegas was a fucking fluke. I made a mistake, but it wasn't in taking you to bed. No, my mistake was in rushing it. You deserve time. This body needs time to come apart." He fingered her nipple and caressing down to her hips.

She whimpered. Eva didn't know how long she was going to last with his determination. Her body was already on fire and burning brighter than it ever had before. She was melting inside and out.

"By the time we leave this room everyone will know I've made amends."

Eva cried out as he pulled out of her pussy. Seconds later his lips replaced his cock. Going to her elbows she watched him lick her pussy. He circled her bud then licked down to slam inside her cunt. Tiny fucked her with his tongue then slid up to stroke her clit.

She couldn't contain her screams as he was relentless in his assault.

"Come for me, baby," he said.

Three fingers entered her as he sucked her clit into his mouth. Eva splintered apart, screaming out her release. He held her hips, licking, sucking and drawing her orgasm out. There was nothing else for her to do other than give herself over to him. Holding onto the edge of the desk, she moaned as he drove her into a second orgasm.

Eva was coming down from her second orgasm as he thrust inside her. His cock was big and wide. He filled her completely. His hands were back on her hips.

She held onto his arms as he pulled out of her only to slam back inside. There was nothing holding him back. He fucked her hard. The desk moved under the weight of his thrusts.

He picked her up, sitting back on his chair with her in his lap. Tiny nipped at her breasts as he pounded inside her. Considering he was a fifty year old man he sure had stamina and knew what he was doing.

Tiny pounded away inside her, hitting her cervix

that had her gasping for more. She held onto the back of his chair as he completely took over her body. In that instant, Eva didn't feel conscious of her weight. Some of the sweet-butts who stuck around the compound ready to screw any member were slender without an ounce of fat on them. She had curves and then some. Her body jiggled, and every part of her was natural.

"So fucking tight," he said, growling. He pushed the hair of her neck and brought her in close. Seconds later she felt his lips sucking at her neck, marking her skin. "Everyone is going to know who owns you. You're fucking mine, Eva."

She'd never heard him be so possessive before. It was like another man was stood in his place even though she knew it was Tiny.

"My woman. I'll kill any man who puts his hands on you," he said.

"Shut up. No talking." She couldn't listen to him. Nothing he said was going to make her stay. They were not for life. Too much had passed between them to make her stay with him.

In a swift movement they were out of the chair, and she was laid on his carpet with him hovering over her. He lifted her legs over his shoulders and found his way back inside her. She tensed feeling the stirring of another orgasm fast approaching. There was nothing left for her to do other than to give him what he wanted. This was about Tiny. He'd already made up for their time together. There was no way she was ever going to forget about this. They'd come too far together for her to give this up.

"So fucking good," he said, slamming inside her.

She saw where they were joined, and the pleasure consumed her. Sinking her fingers into the carpet, she cried out as he hit a part of her that sent her spiraling into another orgasm. His fingers stroked her clit prolonging her release. She'd never had an orgasm with a cock inside her. The feeling was so different as he pounded inside her.

Eva moaned, loving the way he possessed and owned her. He wrapped her legs around his waist and surrounded her. His arms were thick and showcased his strength with the definition of his muscles.

"I've got you, Eva," he said.

There was something in his voice that made her sense a change within him. He wasn't just saying that for her. Tiny didn't say stuff he didn't mean. What had changed?

She didn't know the answer but held onto him all the same.

His pace slowed down, and for the first time in her life, Eva knew what it felt like to be made love to.

He kissed her lips and stroked her body. Tiny went slow showing her everything he could do. She hoped this wasn't some payback for what she'd said in her drunken state many nights ago.

His fingers were tangled in her hair as he made love. He rolled over, and she was laid on top of him. Sitting up, she gazed down at him confused.

"I want to see your tits bouncing. Ride my cock, Eva."

Tiny squeezed her hips, and she knew there would be bruises come the morning. He set the pace letting her know what he wanted. She gave it to him, riding his cock as he caressed her body.

He was big, and she took him deep. Tiny used her hips to bring her down hard on his shaft. He cursed and growled as she fucked him. She felt desired and powerful, holding onto his abdomen as they made love.

She was surprised to see he still had his jeans

around his ankles, but they hadn't moved much from their position.

"Touch yourself," he said.

Opening her eyes she stared down at him. Pressing her fingers to his lips he licked her fingers. She touched her clit and held back a moan. Eva felt sensitive all over from the smallest touches. "That's it. I want to feel you come all over my cock again."

His voice was gruff, and she knew he was hanging on by a thread. She didn't want that. With her free hand she caressed his balls reaching behind her to stroke him at the same time.

"What are you doing?" he asked, moaning.

"I want you to come." She rode his body, and how she managed to do all three things amazed her. Her need overrode everything else, including common sense.

He thrust up to meet her, matching her need with his own. Together they crashed toward their orgasm. She felt and heard his release as he pounded inside her. His cock jerked and pulsed his seed inside her.

She was aware of the lack of protection. Collapsing onto his body from her fourth orgasm, Eva didn't care. One time shouldn't be a big deal. Deep down in her own mind she knew all it took was one time, but nothing was going to spoil her moment with Tiny.

This was the only time she saw him vulnerable. His hands surrounded her holding her close.

"Am I hurting you?" she asked. Her ear was to his chest, and she listened to the rapid beating of his heart start to slow down.

"No, you're perfect, Eva." He kissed the top of her hand.

Tiny stroked her back, and she closed her eyes basking in their closeness. She couldn't allow herself to give in to what he wanted. His relationship with his first wife hadn't been all it was made out to be. Patricia had been his rock, but there had been problems. From what she'd been told from the first moment Tiny saw Patricia he'd been in love with her. At first, their marriage had been perfect, and it was only over time, after Tate was born, that things started to get difficult. In the beginning Tiny had been intent on making Fort Wills into the town it was today. He'd been protecting Patricia from his past. Something had happened to Tiny in Fort Wills before he met his first wife. Alex told her all about it one night. The other man didn't blame Tiny for what happened. Nothing could stop cancer, and she knew Tiny had loved his wife.

In his own way, Tiny had saved the town and Patricia.

She tucked some hair behind her ear as reality started to set in. Not only was reality starting to set in but also the sounds of everyone moving around in the other room. Her father was coming at the end of the week to pick her up.

Sitting up she felt Tiny tighten his hold around her. "We don't have to leave. The baby shower is not for a couple of days. No one needs us."

"I've got to help organize everything," she said, sitting up. His cock twitched and started to harden once again. "Are you never satisfied?"

"Around you, no."

She smiled and looked down at the names within his tattoo. The names showed his true nature, the caring man he tried to keep hidden from everyone.

He caught her hand as she made to touch the names. "Don't," he said.

"Why do you keep yourself away from everyone?" she asked, struck by how isolated he made himself.

"People die, and people get killed. I'm not going to risk getting close to people who died." His hands touched her shoulder where the scar from the bullet she'd taken still lay. "You could have been killed because of me. I can't let that happen."

"So you screw women you don't care about to throw off the scent of you actually being a decent human being."

He grabbed both of her arms tight, sitting up. "Never make the mistake of thinking I'm a decent human being, Eva. I'm not. I've done shit that will make you sick to your stomach."

"Everyone has a past, Tiny. You're just too afraid to share yours." She pushed him away and climbed off his lap. Their moment together had been short and sweet, but she wasn't about to play twenty questions and try to get him to open up.

Tiny was a complicated man, but she knew far more than he realized.

"Fuck, Eva, stop. This is not what I had planned."

She found her dress and started to work it back on. Her panties were ruined. Eva didn't even bother to search for her bra. "No, you wanted to wipe the memory of Vegas, fine. It's done. You're a fuck machine and great at it." She quickly got dressed putting her heels on. "I can take a lot of crap, Tiny. Keeping me off limits to your life while fucking me is not one of them. If you wanted me then I'd be by your side, and everyone would know it. Yes, you've got a past, but so have fucking I. I'm not some sweet little girl, Tiny. I was never one of them. That woman you knew wasn't the true me. I've never been sweet."

"Eva, wait," he said.

Turning on her heel she made her way for the door. She didn't care what people thought of her.

Hearing him fumble around she didn't give him chance to stop her. Unlocking the door she left the room. Several of the men saw her leave. They didn't say anything to her, but she knew what they were thinking. The interest in their eyes was hard to ignore. Walking out of the door, she heard Tiny call her name. She didn't stop and kept walking. Alex was stood by his car smoking a cigarette.

"Will you take me home?" she asked.

"Alex, don't you fucking dare." The tarmac surface must be stopping Tiny. When she looked back she saw him getting closer.

"Sure," Alex said, climbing into the car. In the wing mirror she watched Tiny try to stop her. Nothing more was to be done. At the end of the week she'd be out of his life and wouldn't look back.

****

Killer stood outside of Kelsey's apartment building hoping to catch her on her way home. He would have waited outside of work, but the women were not particularly nice to her, and when he'd threatened to hurt them, Kelsey hadn't been happy with it. She wanted nothing to do with him or The Skulls, which he understood. But he knew he could make her happy no matter what she said.

The attacks on the women had finally turned Kelsey away from him. Their relationship hadn't been the best considering they'd first met when they were being attacked by a fucking drug gang.

Some of the Fort Wills women passed him giggling. They were blonde and slender, pushing their breasts out to try to catch his attention. He wasn't interested in any woman other than Kelsey. From the first moment he saw her, he'd been struck dumb. She was everything he'd ever wanted in a woman. Kelsey was sweet, intelligent, and she was a fucking dental nurse as well. He loved to spend his time watching her. Nothing else had to happen. He'd gladly watch her. When he spotted her coming around the corner he tensed. Her cherry blonde hair fell around her shoulders in waves as her head was bowed while she watched the floor in front of her.

He found it adorable how she never looked up to see who was watching her. She didn't have any clue how beautiful she was.

"Kelsey," he said, calling her name.

She jerked and looked in his direction. Her eyes were a beautiful shade of blue. He felt his cock harden at the sight of her alone. Even surrounded in a coat he knew she had a sexy body to go with her face. He'd not seen her completely naked, but he'd seen enough to know what he liked.

"Theo, what are you doing here?" she asked.

Wincing at the name, Killer left his bike. His real name was Theodore Smith. No one was afraid by a man with such a name, and The Lions had renamed him Killer.

"I wanted to come and see you to make sure you were all right." He hadn't come to see if she was all right.

She may think they were over, but it was far from over for him. He wanted her too damn much to let it be over.

"I'm fine. Everything is fine. Work is the same." She stood with her arms folded. Her bag was over her shoulder, and he remembered her buying it in town. Why was he thinking about her fucking bag? There was so much he wanted to say.

"Tate misses you. She doesn't invite you back to the club because she knows you'll refuse," he said. Bringing Tate into the conversation was a low blow, but he had to play it as otherwise Kelsey was gone.

"I miss her, too." She dropped her hands and stared at him. "What is this about?"

He closed the distance between them. Wrapping his fingers around the back of her neck, he forced her to look at him. "This is not over."

"Theo—"

"No, my name is Killer. Use it."

"This is not how this works. We're not the same." Her palm was pressed to his shirt front.

"Is this about your education and the fact I've got none?"

"What? No. How could you even think that?" she asked. Tears filled her eyes as she looked at him.

"I've not taken another woman since I met you, Kels. This is not over." He couldn't hold back any longer and slammed his lips down on hers.

Love, lust, pure craving filled him at the feel of her lips underneath his. With one hand wrapped around the back of her neck, he used the other to cup her ass. He wasn't letting her go.

She gasped, opening her lips. He took full advantage, plundering his tongue inside. Her gasp turned to a moan. Killer felt her melt against him like she had so many times before. He imagined her pussy must be flowing with arousal. They'd never gotten that close to each other.

Kelsey was the first woman he'd ever known to keep her clothes on at all times. She wouldn't let him take her to bed. Everything was not about sex and fucking. She was the first woman to ever ask him how he was. Didn't she realize how fucking important she was to him?

"No," she said, pushing away. "I can't do this."

He refused to let her go.

"Why?" he asked, feeling anger once again at being pushed aside. "Tell me why?"

The tears that had filled her eyes finally fell onto her cheeks. "I'm not strong enough for this. Tate, Angel, they're strong for you being who you are. They stand by their men. I can't do this. I can't be with you or give myself to you. It's too much, and I'm not who you think I am. I'm not strong."

With her words hanging in the air, she turned on her heel and ran.

Killer watched her go feeling his whole world leave him. Kelsey was also the first woman he'd ever loved.

Chapter Three

Tiny was livid. The pale cream and pink did nothing to relieve his anger as he stared around the compound. He wore no shirt, and he'd just watched Alex take his woman away in a car. He knew where they were going, yet his anger refused to cease. His men were laughing and drinking beer as the women fussed around the room. The sight of pink made him feel sick.

Tate walked up to him, smiling. Her smiling face was the only thing that could defuse him.

"Daddy, I love you, but you need to do up your pants."

He'd been in a rush to get to Eva when he saw her leaving, and he'd not given any thought to his state of undress. His shoes and the rest of his clothes were still in his office. The scent of Eva's release surrounded him.

Quickly zipping up his pants, Tiny cursed. "When your Uncle gets back, he's a dead man."

"No, he's not. You love Uncle Alex like a brother. Besides, him taking Eva away is probably the best." Tate was flicking through a catalogue with babies on the cover.

"And why is that?" he asked, getting annoyed again.

"You've said something to make her run from you. When it comes to Eva you're always saying or doing something to piss her off. I'm surprised she has stayed so long." She looked up from out of the catalogue. "You don't think she's going to be waiting around forever, do you?"

"Do you have a problem with her?"

"No. I love Eva. Always have and always will. My love of her is not going to stop her from leaving," Tate said, folding her arms over her chest.

"She's not leaving. Eva is staying in Fort Wills."

Tate scoffed. "You're like every other man. Murphy thought he could tame me, and yet he's still trying." She tapped Tiny on the shoulder. "Dream on, Dad."

She walked away before he could refute her statement. Fucking women, even his daughter was plotting against him, but she got her attitude from him, which he couldn't complain about. He watched her go to Angel and Sophia. All three women were pregnant with his men's babies. The next generation meant a lot to him. Without the future of The Skulls there would be no one to keep Fort Wills safe. They all had a responsibility to the town to protect them all. He took his job very seriously as a protector.

"They all look happy, don't they?" Zero asked, stepping up beside him.

"If you're going to make some fucking snide comment about what went down in the office then we can take this outside."

"I've got nothing to say about Eva or the noises she makes."

Tiny tensed. He saw Zero wasn't looking at him but at the women giggling. Nash moved behind Sophia to stroke her waist. The other Skull was the only guy in the room with a bottle of water in his hand. He was proud Nash was taking his addictions seriously. Sophia was good for the other man. She kept him grounded.

The way Eva grounds you.

Another one of his thoughts, he cut off quickly. He couldn't be thinking about himself and Eva together or how she completed him and made him want to be a better man.

"You're not poaching on another woman, are you?"

They all worked by knowing the women who were taken and the women who were fair game.

"No, I'm not taking Nash's woman. Sophia's … I don't know. She's different, yet she's the same. It's like a part of her refuses to see all the shit that goes on, and she's been dealt shit and knows it exists. I respect her, okay. It's not often you'll hear me say that about a woman."

"I take it you've been bitten by the woman bug?"

"No, I just know women are not always the best source of company," Zero said.

"That's wonderful to know, Zero," Sandy said. Sandy was the resident doctor.

Tiny saw the anger in the woman's eyes, and it was all directed at Zero.

In the last month Sandy had started hanging around the compound more often. From what he heard no man was getting between her thighs anymore. Tiny knew it had something to do with the stabbing over Nash. She'd been in a coma for a few days, and it had been touch and go over her life.

"You're different, Sandy," Zero said, trying to make up for his words.

"I sleep with men who don't give a fuck about commitment, but that doesn't mean I wouldn't be faithful to the right man." She glared daggers at Zero before turning her gaze to him. "I need to talk with you."

He motioned toward his office. There was no exotic sway to her hips as he followed behind her. Tiny stared at Sandy's back and noticed she wore more clothes than he'd ever seen on her. She wore jeans and a long sweater. Her hair was pulled back into a ponytail. He saw she looked younger than her forty years. He'd fucked her once many months ago. Afterwards he'd not been able to go home to Eva for the shame that consumed him.

They'd not even been dating, but he felt the betrayal.

You're not even dating now.

Closing the door he walked to his desk. The computer was fried and was no way to get repaired. He'd have to get a new one. "What can I do for you?" he asked.

She bent down to help pick up everything he and Eva had spilled to the floor.

"You don't need to help with that," he said, taking the paperwork off her hands.

Sandy took a seat, and he lowered himself down into his own. He couldn't believe less than an hour ago he'd been fucking Eva in the very same chair. The room smelled like sex to him. It was a good smell, and he didn't care if Sandy smelled it or not.

"I know I'm not one of your men or part of the club—"

"You're part of the club, Sandy. What happened to you should never have happened. Don't think that you're not appreciated because you are. You mean a lot to me and the club."

She looked down at her lap. He saw her hands were gripping her knees tightly.

"I, erm, I quit work at the hospital."

He listened, shocked by the fact she quit work.

"I handed in my notice, and I'm finished with the place. I can't go home. Being alone hurts, but I can't be with any of the men either." She looked up at him. He saw the tears spilling from her eyes. "I've never felt this way before. I'm alone. I've got no family. I was a doctor, and I loved the life within the club but … I can't do it."

She wiped at her eyes. "I thought about leaving, and I got in my car to leave. There's nowhere for me to go. I can't support myself."

"Do you need money?" he asked.

"No, this is not about money. What I'm asking is can I stay here? I can pay rent or something. Can I stay here without being with one of the men? I don't want to be an old lady or anyone's woman. I just want to be left alone to deal."

The desperation in her voice cut him deep. She'd been one of the only women who didn't have a prospect on her, and she'd suffered because of it. No one would have hurt her if he'd thought ahead.

Getting up from his seat, he walked to the door. "Stink, come here."

He waited by his door for the other brother to walk into the room. Stink didn't have any sense of smell. The other man did all the shit jobs without a problem. He was sure it would only be a matter of time before the boys renamed him when they grew tired of calling him Stink.

"Yes, boss," Stink said, entering the room.

Tiny told him everything with Sandy. He knew the other man wouldn't even try it on with her and with the right order, would protect Sandy with his life. Stink once confided in him that he wasn't interested in quick easy fucks with Sandy. Stink wanted forever and had the biggest crush on her. No one within the club knew it apart from him. Sandy and Stink would make a good team for now. Tiny knew that Stink wouldn't do anything to hurt Sandy or put moves on her.

"Are you okay with this arrangement?" Tiny asked, looking at Sandy. The other woman stared at Stink.

"He knows I'm not interested in anything else?"

"Babe, I'm not going to touch you other than to be your bodyguard and safety net. I've no interest in bedding you."

If Tiny didn't know better he'd say Stink had his

fingers crossed behind his back.

"Okay, then I'm good with this, Tiny." Sandy got up from her seat. "Thank you for being so considerate."

She placed a cool hand on his arm.

Closing the door Tiny remembered a long time ago when he'd turned and walked away from a woman to be hurt.

The memory swamped him, threatening to drag him down.

****

Tiny, before The Skulls began

Tiny stared around the grounds. Mikey stood smoking a cigarette. The look of disgust on the other man's face scared him. Fort Wills was a fucking shit hole, and no one cared about what went on in the little town off the beaten track. No one visited unless they wanted to end up dead or as part of The Darkness. He heard Snitch laughing his head off in the distance followed by the sound of a feminine cry.

"He's at it again," Mikey said. Devil walked out of the forest carrying a bottle of vodka. They were the only two men Tiny really knew who hated what The Darkness did. The Darkness was a group of thugs who controlled the town. When they told the residents to jump, the town simply asked, how high?

"What?" Tiny asked. Fear filled every corner of his soul at the desperate screams.

"He's raping another girl. They're all fucking monsters," Mikey said.

Devil threw his bottle against the tree. In the last few months, The Darkness had gotten out of control. There was once a time when Tiny loved being part of a strong group of men. They fucked whoever they wanted and beat the shit out of anyone who stood in their way. If there was order, they would make it their mission to fuck it over.

*"I'm many things, but I'm not a fucking rapist,"
Devil said. "I'm out of here. I'm done."*

*"You can't just walk away," Tiny said, holding
his ground. They were all in this together.*

*Devil moved forward. The scent of alcohol made
Tiny's stomach roll. "Tell you what, Tiny, go and see
what they're doing, and you tell me what you're going to
do."*

*Looking back at Mikey, he saw the pain on the
older man's face. Mikey was only a few years old than he
was, but he'd clearly seen too much crap.*

*Stumbling across the uneven ground, Tiny went
toward the group. Snitch, the town leader and thug, was
pumping away between a woman's thighs. What he saw
would stay with him forever. Tiny grabbed his gun and
stared at what was going on. The girl on the ground was
someone's daughter or wife or even girlfriend. She meant
something to someone, and they were using her like a rag
doll. He saw the tears mixed with the snot.*

*Aiming the gun he was prepared to fight. He had
to save the girl from what they were doing to her. Tiny
knew what was going to happen, and it sickened him.
They were going to take turns. How long had this been
going on? Where the fuck had he been when this started
happening?*

*"If you pull that trigger we're all dead," Devil
said, catching him unaware. The other man and Mikey
had snuck up on him.*

*The gun was taken off him. Tiny didn't know who
by, only that it was taken from him. The two men led him
out from the scene into the clearing.*

*He bent over and vomited everything he'd ever
eaten. Fuck, what the hell was the world coming to? His
world was awful. There was no one to protect and*

everything to destroy. The girl's pain had been written all over her face. No one was going to stop them.

"We have to go back and help her," Tiny said, pleading with the others.

"There are more than ten men back there. You start shooting, you're going to end up dead, the girl, too."

"She's dying anyway," Mikey said. "There's nothing we can do."

"It's time I was going. I never liked this place much, and if I ever touch a woman who doesn't want it, I want fucking shooting." Devil stood up. "If you ever need me contact me."

Tiny watched the other man leave.

"You can stop this," Mikey said.

"How?"

"By fighting back."

Tiny had fought back. He sent Snitch and The Darkness out of Fort Wills. A lot of men lost their lives when he did. He'd buried them and hadn't shed a tear when he'd done it. The following morning he'd gone back to the place they'd used the girl. Someone had shot her, leaving her to bleed out. He'd never known her name, but he'd taken the time to bury her and give her a headstone. She was laid in the Fort Wills cemetery as a constant reminder of what he couldn't do and what he was determined to change in the town.

****

Eva placed the final dress into the suitcase. She had a handful of clothes ready for the couple of days to go. The purple dress for the baby shower was hung in her wardrobe along with some jeans and shirts. Everything else was packed, ready for her father to pick her up on Friday.

She heard the door opening and closing.

Staring at the cases, she waited for Tiny to make an appearance in her doorway. She still wore the blue dress from that morning.

When the door opened she turned to look at him. Frowning, she saw he looked in pain.

"You're still leaving?" he asked.

"Nothing is going to stop me leaving."

He was leaning against the doorframe staring at her. Tiny looked ill as if he was going to vomit at any moment.

"The Skulls didn't always run this town," he said, stepping into the room. She tensed, waiting for him to continue. "This place was a fucking shit place to live. The town was shit with no order. There were no cops. Well, there were cops, but they were fucking useless, and no one gave a shit."

"What's this all about?" she asked, stepping in front of him.

"There were a lot of problems with this place. It was run by a small group known as The Darkness, a group of thugs and fucking criminals. I don't know why no one ever cared about this fucking place. We must have slipped out of caring or something."

Eva knew this place had been a nightmare. Her father and many of the fighters who worked for him had heard about this place. The reason she'd chosen to come here trying to get away from her father was because it would be the last place he'd look to find her.

"What was The Darkness?" she asked.

He started laughing. "It sounds like a fucking rock group. It wasn't. Far from it. The concept was when you met one of us, all you'd see is darkness. You'd be dead."

She understood the term. "You were young then?"

"Yeah, I was young, foolish and a fucking idiot." He was silent for many minutes. "There is shit you don't know about me, and I never want you to learn the truth. I can't tell you everything. I will not relive it for you."

Eva wanted to ask so many questions. Instead, she sat beside him. Taking his hand, she locked their fingers together.

"What happened to them?"

"To who?" he asked.

"The Darkness. A group like that doesn't just disappear." She knew he would have killed some of them to get Fort Wills the way it was. Eva also knew that some of the men wouldn't have left easily.

"Who we didn't kill left."

"It's strange," she said.

"What's strange?" he asked.

"A group as powerful as that, why did they leave and not come back, trying to get what they lost?" She was thinking out loud.

"A lot of them were killed. The ones that left would know not to come back. Anyone with sense wouldn't try to fight for what they couldn't win back. They're gone, and for Fort Wills's sake, they better never come back."

Getting up from the bed, she left him alone, heading downstairs. She'd put a small chicken in the oven so they could pick over the meat for some sandwiches.

"Why did you leave?" he asked, standing in the kitchen.

"I always leave. You never say much before it's time for me to go." She shrugged. They had a really difficult relationship. There were times she was sure they were making progress, and at other times she felt like they were taking a step back. She wasn't prepared to give into his demands. They had sex but that didn't mean a commitment to her. Tiny had a long way to go before she'd ever consider forever with him. She didn't trust him around other women, and he never made a commitment to her.

"Tonight, can we have tonight where we don't talk about the club or what we've got to do?" he asked.

She placed the roast chicken on top of the stove and stared at him. Her pussy was tender from their fucking. Staring at his graying hair, Eva felt an answering arousal start within her.

"Nothing is going to change what's going to happen. On Friday, my father is taking me home."

"I know." He stood opposite her, staring. "I'm asking for tonight."

He wouldn't beg. It wasn't his style.

"Fine. We've got tonight." She dealt with the chicken as he circled the counter. Before she knew what he was doing, his hand was under the skirt of her dress.

"Good. I want you naked now."

Eva placed their chicken down while Tiny tore the dress from her shoulders. Growling in anger, Eva heard the fabric tear. "Be patient," she said.

"No. I don't give a fuck about eating." He moved her to a clean surface and pressed on her back until her breasts were on the counter. She squeaked from the cold.

The sound of his zipper opening met her ears. In the next instance his cock found her pussy and thrust to the hilt. He moaned as she curled her toes to stop herself from making a noise. He was large, and she'd not been prepared for the penetration.

"I know that hurt you. I'm sorry, baby. I needed to feel your cunt around my dick." He stroked her clit. Within moments she felt herself responding to him. "You're ready for me now."

He pulled out of her body only to slam back inside. There was no give in him. He was a force to be reckoned with. Holding onto the edge of the counter she cried out as his wet fingers circled her anus. She'd never had her ass touched, and the sensation was entirely sensual.

"Is this about Vegas?" she asked, looking at him over her shoulder. His gaze was smoldering. She felt scolded just by looking at him.

"No. I don't give a fuck about Vegas. This is you and me and what I should have done years ago." He slapped her ass, tightened his hands on her hips, and pounded into her in three quick thrusts. "Such a pretty ass." He slapped her ass again before she felt his fingers back to her asshole.

Tensing, she looked across the room, waiting for what he was going to do.

"Open for me, baby. I can give this to you." He pressed the tip of his finger to her ass.

She tightened her body not wanting him inside. Yet, even though she didn't want him inside she didn't stop him either. She felt conflicted inside over what she wanted and what she didn't.

His other hand delved between her thighs, and he started to stroke her clit. Biting her lip, she struggled underneath him.

"You're going to open up to me, baby. You're mine. I own every inch of you."

He did, but she was never going to let him know the truth.

Fighting against him, Eva knew it was useless. Her body was already opening beneath him.

Relaxing against his hold, she held her breath. The tip of his finger worked past her muscles. Slowly, he slid his finger in deep.

"You're a fucking virgin, aren't you, baby?"

Shaking her head, she kept her eyes closed.

His hand that had been between her thighs fisted her hair. He tugged on the length forcing her to look at him at an odd angle.

"Answer me," he said.

"No, no one has been there."

"Good. I'm taking that all for myself."

Refuse him. Tell him no.

She kept her lips shut and her words of denial to herself. Tiny could have any part of her, but she would not give him everything. When she first met him as a young girl she would have been a fool and offered him everything on a plate. Now, after the time they'd been together, Eva knew he would only hurt her more. She couldn't afford to give him her heart and soul.

He was like the men she'd run from. Her father's fighters were of a similar mind, using women for pleasure.

Cutting off the thoughts of her past she moaned as his finger penetrated her ass, working her over. The pain and pleasure mixed together catching her unaware. She felt her arousal flooding her pussy and spreading down her thighs.

"I'll take my sweet time taking your ass, Eva."

No words were necessary as in the next breath he pulled out of her pussy only to slam back inside. Holding onto the counter she did her best to stay still. Tiny was not a small man or a weak man. He possessed a lot of strength behind his thick corded muscles.

"Let me hear your moans. I want to hear your pleasure, Eva. Give it to me."

She sank her teeth into her lip denying him her pleasure.

Slap.

Slap.
Slap.

With the feel of his palm on her ass and the sting from his spanks, Eva could no longer keep her sounds to herself. Releasing her lip she cried out, groaning as his other hand returned to her clit.

"That's it, baby. Show me how much you love my cock. You're so fucking wet. Your cream is coating my dick." He thrust into her in six hard thrusts, stroking her clit.

She splintered apart coming over him once again.

"Good girl. Let's see how you take a second finger."

He touched her ass, wiggling his finger, stretching her open. The hand between her thighs returned to her hip. She couldn't move. The strength he had kept her firmly in place. Tiny could seriously hurt her, and it wouldn't take him much to do.

The fact his hands caressed her rather than hurt her made Eva feel better.

"Fuck, your ass is tight. I'm going to have to work this ass to get what I want."

Still Eva remained silent.

His second finger opened her up. The pain confused her even though pleasure struck every sensory nerve she possessed. Tiny knew what he was doing to her. He was clearly confident in what her body needed. How was she going to walk away come Friday?

Eva didn't know the answer to that question, only that she had to in order to save her a lot of heartache.

Chapter Four

Eva took his fingers, and he sawed them together, opening up her ass. He'd never known a woman to be so fucking tight. Most of the women he knew were sweet-butts who were used to be taken in every orifice.

Only he would be the one to take full possession of Eva. She wasn't a virgin, but her ass was untouched, and he intended to take it. Pumping his fingers into her ass he felt her cunt ripple around him.

He loved this woman and had been in love with her for a long time. No matter what he felt for her, he wouldn't give in to the need. Being the leader, the boss of The Skulls, stopped him from letting himself be that vulnerable. Patricia had protection in her brother and had died of cancer. She broke his heart when she died. They'd had their problems, but he really did love her. He would still be with her now if she was alive. But Eva *was* alive, breathing, and had the power to shatter every part of him.

Holding himself back was the only way he knew he'd be able to survive the danger of what Eva could cause him. Lash, Murphy, and Nash had all faced their woman being hurt. Seeing Eva shot and knowing he was the one responsible tore at him. He'd already seen one of his women being taken from him. Tiny knew deep down that he couldn't live through Eva being taken either.

No, he wouldn't be openly claiming Eva as his woman. Only the club would know what she meant to him.

Tiny stopped himself from thinking about the life outside the door. This was the life he chose, and he wouldn't be stopping it any time soon.

Turning his fingers, he stared at where his cock was buried in her pussy. Her lips opened around him.

The image was so erotic he felt his balls tighten getting ready to explode inside her. There was no condom between them. He didn't want the latex to obscure anything.

He couldn't even bring himself to give a fuck if she got pregnant. The only thing he knew in that single moment was how damn hot she felt naked for him.

"You want me to fuck you, don't you, baby?"

"Tiny, fuck me, or leave me to finish off what you started."

She was panting. With one hand on her hip he watched his dick leave her pussy until only the tip remained inside her. His shaft was wet with her arousal.

In one quick thrust he fucked inside her. He couldn't wait any longer. Tiny needed to orgasm, or he wouldn't make it through the night. Alternating his thrusts between taking her pussy and then slamming his fingers into her ass, Tiny worked up a steady rhythm opening her up for him.

Fucking her hard, Tiny tensed as his balls tightened. His release was close, and with two final thrusts inside her pussy the wash of pleasure swept over him.

Moaning, he held onto her tight with his fingers in deep into her ass. She groaned letting him do what he wanted.

When it was over, he removed his fingers from her ass. Reaching over her head, he cleaned his fingers on the damp towel. She tried to move, and he steadied her.

"Wait. I'm not finished with you yet."

Eva paused underneath him. Cleaning his hand and then her ass, Tiny took his time. He expected her to argue with him or at least curse him. She remained bent over the counter.

"I don't want you to move," he said.

"I get it, Tiny. Stay still until you've had your fun. I get it. I understand, stay still."

He slapped her ass. "Sarcasm doesn't suit you."

"Bite me!"

"Oh, baby, I certainly will, just not tonight." Tiny waited until he knew she was going to stay still.

When she showed no intention of moving, he slowly withdrew from her pussy. Opening the lips of her sex he stared at her. She was flushed from his cock, red and puffy at the same time. Then he saw his own cum at her entrance starting to leave her body. Something primitive caught him, holding him in place like he held Eva in place.

He never once considered himself possessive, but when it came to Eva, he was. Seeing his cum flooding her cunt turned him on. Even after finding orgasm minutes before, he felt a stirring in his gut.

"Are you doing what I think you're doing?" she asked.

Standing over her, he pressed his fingers into her pussy stopping his cum from leaking out of her. "I'm watching my cum in your body."

"Pervert."

"When it comes to you, yes." He fingered her pussy, and she shook underneath him. As he kissed her neck, Eva relaxed underneath him. "I'm going to fill every part of you, Eva."

"Why?" she asked. The confusion was clear to hear in her voice.

"Because I can. You've given yourself to me, and if you don't stick around come Friday, I know you won't be able to forget about me." He was a bastard, but he didn't care. Eva was the only person he wanted, and the woman beneath him was going to realize when it came to her, he didn't play fair and would never play fair. "You like what I'm doing to you."

She didn't dispute him. Eva remained still as he worked his cum back inside. Moving her hair out of the way, he sucked on her neck going around then down her back, dropping little kisses. He'd not shaved in a day, and the bristles left red marks on her flesh.

Satisfied that he'd worked her up once again, Tiny withdrew his hand going toward the sink.

Turning back he saw she was in the position he'd left her. "You may get up now and fix us some food."

"You're a fucking bastard," she said, standing up tall.

She was completely naked, and this time he got to really look at her. Dropping the towel he'd been using to dry his hands, he crossed the distance to her. Eva hadn't moved from her spot near the counters. Picking her up with his arm around her waist, he placed her on the hard, cold surface.

"You better believe it, baby. Tonight you're mine, and I'm not holding back. I'm the fucking boss. I'm in charge, and you'll do as you're told."

Sinking his fingers into her hair, he tugged her close, slamming his lips onto hers. "You're not going to get everything you want that easily," she said, fighting him as he claimed her lips. They were laughing together. The passion changed between them, turning into something more playful. Eva was a little hell cat, and he loved the challenge of taming her. No, he didn't want to tame her at all. Her fire when he first saw it surprised him. Their time in Vegas had awakened her fire. Since her time away even though it was a few hours she'd changed. It was like her being back home had showed her that she'd been changing and not for the good. He always thought she was sweet, innocent, untouchable.

Then she'd come home and defied him at every turn, showing him she was far from sweet and innocent. At times he still felt she was untouchable. Eva was good from the inside out. No one deserved her, but he sure as hell was going to try. Her giggles stopped as she looked him in the eye seeing his seriousness.

Plundering her mouth, he stroked over her tongue with his.

He pressed a final kiss to her lips. "Do you have a problem?"

As he ran his hands up her thighs, his cock stirred, wanting inside her.

She didn't say anything. Her gaze shot daggers at him even as her lips were turned upwards.

"I'm being nice, Eva." Drawing her to the edge, he pressed his cock to her entrance and forged his way inside. "You see, I want you now, but I'm being nice in letting you have some food. You won't be getting any sleep any time soon. You're mine, baby. Tonight I intend to use you as mine. I'll keep telling you until you realize the truth."

He pumped into her a couple of times. She started to relent, and he left her body once again. "Now be a good girl and make us some food." He stepped back aware of his cock standing tall, proud and wanting back inside her wet warmth.

She climbed off the side, glaring at him.

Her hazel depths were fucking tempting. Watching her, he admired the curves of her body. There were no bones protruding out, which always left him wanting to give the woman a hot meal. Her body had real flesh for him to hold onto. Being the big man with the strength he knew he possessed, thin women were always a challenge to him.

When he was with skinny women he held himself

back for fear of hurting them. He loved good sex, hard sex, and he did have it with slender women, but part of him always made sure not to let go. The times he'd been with Eva he hadn't held back.

She was strong and took his passion.

"I've got to go to the office. I'll be back in a few minutes."

Eva didn't say anything and kept making sandwiches. Something she'd spoken of earlier had stuck with him. Snitch hadn't been killed all those years ago. At least, he hadn't been killed by his hand. Closing his office door, he went to the picture on the far wall and removed it. Entering the correct code in the secure safe, he opened the door. Several guns lay on a stack of cash. Eva knew the code. After the break in from The Lions, he'd made sure to train her with a gun in their free time. Along the side were all the files he possessed. The ones he kept at home were all the important files that he didn't want anyone to know about. He trusted Eva. Maybe he was a fucking idiot for doing it, but he did trust her.

Grabbing the file, he closed the safe, replaced the mirror and sat behind his desk. Turning on the light, he flicked the file open to see a picture of Snitch staring back at him. If the man survived the takeover of Fort Wills then he'd be a couple of years older than Tiny. The thought of Snitch out there worried Tiny. The other man didn't give a fuck about anyone but vengeance. Why wait twenty years to make his move? Unless Snitch had to start from scratch with building up his club. A lot of men were killed in the takeover of Fort Wills. Not many men made it out alive.

Picking up his phone he dialed Devil's number. He always knew how to keep in touch with the other man. It was part of their agreement. Devil didn't want to stay behind in Fort Wills. He helped to get Snitch out of town, but he didn't stay to take over.

"What?" Devil asked.

Tiny heard the music playing over the phone. Whistles, catcalls, and all sorts of noises came over the line.

"Are you able to talk?" Tiny rubbed at his temple.

"I've got plenty of naked girls around me, Tiny. I don't think your guys were right about the sister. I can't fucking find her." Devil sounded annoyed yet distracted.

"My boys are not wrong. If you can't find her then she doesn't want to be found. My boys gave you the location for her sister. Stop looking for the mother of your kid, and start looking for her sister." Tiny flicked through the file wishing he didn't have to open it up.

"I'll find her. You're not the type of man to steer me wrong, and if you do, friend or not, I'll fucking kill you."

Tiny considered it a compliment to be worth killing from Devil.

"She's there."

"What do you want? I take it this is not a social call unless that little blonde bombshell wants to hook up," Devil said, talking about Angel.

"Angel's pregnant with Lash's baby."

"I'm not picky. I'll still take her in."

Shaking his head, Tiny leaned back in his chair. "Did you kill Snitch?"

Silence descended over the line.

"Shit, like that is over twenty years old. Leave it alone," Devil said.

"What if he's back?" Tiny stood going to his window to look out at the dark night. Eva couldn't have been right, but the attack where the thugs took Nash made a little more sense this way. Also, the attack on the women made a lot of sense if Snitch and a new crew were behind it. For some reason Snitch always got people to follow him. The bastard was like the fucking plague.

"Hold on. Get the fuck off me, bitch," Devil said.

Tiny heard a lot of commotion over the line then pure silence as a door closed in the distance. "You've got my attention."

"So you didn't kill him?" Tiny asked.

"I buried a lot of men during that time, Tiny. If you didn't kill him, then Mikey could have or Alex," Devil said.

"Alex wouldn't get his hands dirty, and Mikey would have told me."

"Well if Mikey did kill him he took the info with him to his grave." Devil cursed over the line. "If he's not dead then we're in trouble."

"He's the only person I know who would go after our women," Tiny said. "He doesn't give a shit who gets hurt at all."

"Yeah, if it's him no one is safe. He's a sick fuck. Look, Snitch is an idiot, but he's clever. He will find a way in, Tiny. Watch your back, and keep in fucking touch. Shit, I can't deal with this shit. I gotta find my kid."

"Your kid is with his mother or the sister. He'll be fine."

"The mother is a whore. I'm not leaving my kin with that bitch. I don't even know what her sister is like. Bitch never talked about her. Fuck, I've got to go. One of my boys is calling me." Devil hung up without saying another word.

Placing the phone back into the cradle, Tiny stared at the file he kept on Snitch. It was the one file where his own past blended with that of the other man. There had once been a time when he would have followed this man blindly into anything. The night he watched him gang-rape a girl and torture her had been the final straw for Tiny.

The wakeup call he'd received that night had been a victim too late. If someone ever tried to do that to Tate, he'd castrate the bastard and then take his time killing him.

Running a hand over his face, Tiny felt dread for the first time in over twenty-five years. If Snitch was back then he needed to get his men prepared for the danger coming their way.

****

Several hours later Eva stood washing the dishes. Tiny had banned her from wearing any clothing. Walking around the house butt ass naked was not something she liked doing. Every now and then she caught sight of her body in the mirror. She'd never been one to be overly concerned about her shape. Her father, Ned, taught her at a young age to be proud of who she was, embrace her shape. Smiling, Eva recalled the conversations he tried to have as she was growing.

The first time she got her period would stay with her forever. She'd screamed the entire gym down. At twelve, she thought she was dying. Ned, along with five of his men, charged into the bathroom. The stall had been locked, and the conversation through the metal still made her cringe. The men had laughed at her but promised to be kind now she was a lady.

Shaking her head, Eva picked up a clean towel to dry all the dishes she'd used. None of the men working for her father hurt her either. They made her feel special, but she knew her shape was not for every man. She loved her food, and cooking came naturally to her.

Tiny was still locked away in his office. He joined her for their sandwiches and abandoned her when he finished. Switching off the light she headed upstairs to her room. She tugged each case off her bed, sliding them across the room to her wardrobe. Her time in Tate's and Tiny's lives was coming to an end. She felt it and knew there was no way she could change her mind.

Grabbing her phone, she dialed her father's number.

"Hey, princess, how are you doing? Do you need me to pick you up now?" Ned Walker answered on the first ring. Her father had always been there for her. She felt a little guilty for getting up and leaving him without a word. "I'll be on the first flight out."

"No, Dad, you don't need to come early. I just wanted to make sure you were coming out on Friday. I don't want to be waiting around and you not be here to pick me up."

"Have I ever let you down?" he asked.

Rolling her eyes, she shook her head and then realized he wasn't in the same room. It was a good thing he wasn't in the same room. If he saw her naked he'd kill Tiny on the spot.

"No, you've never let me down."

"Then what is this about? Are you changing your mind?"

"No, it's time for me to come home. Tate is grown up, and I've pissed you off enough."

She sat on the end of the bed wishing she hadn't called him. Ned always did see too much.

"It's not a bad thing to be in love with a man, Eva."

"I know."

"Admittedly, I'd prefer you to be in love with a man your own age, but I guess there are worse men out there. He's … erm … he's not hurting you or anything, is he?"

"What? No, I mean Tiny will hurt anyone who tries to hurt me. He's like you, Dad. Hard yet soft at the same time." She chuckled at his annoyed sigh.

"I'm not soft with anyone else."

The words sobered her up. She knew her father was no saint. He hurt anyone who stood in his path or threatened his family. Eva knew who was responsible for her mother's death, but she wasn't going to get into that. Someone else had told her the truth about her mother a long time ago.

"I know. I need to come away. Clear my head. Everything is always the same at the moment, and I need to know my own mind."

"I'll be there early. I'm catching a flight, but I can't be away too long so don't go changing your mind at the last moment. I've got a fight to get to on Saturday."

"Okay, I'll see you soon. Don't forget to bring three gifts. There are three women expecting."

"You're all breeding like fucking rabbits. Fine, I'll pick something up."

She chuckled before hanging up the phone. She did love and miss her father. He'd stayed away when she asked him to, not wanting him near her when she was in pain. Ned Walker was a force to be reckoned with and would probably make Tiny look like a little teddy bear in comparison.

Leaving the bedroom she took a quick shower to wash away the day. She didn't give a thought about Tiny. Usually when he was locked inside his office there was no chance of him leaving the room for a good few hours.

Eva closed her eyes letting the spray wash over her face and body. She held her neck recalling the feel of Tiny's hands all over her body. His fingers were rough from hard work and made her skin feel so sensitive when he touched her. Every time his palms touched her she felt owned by him. She never knew touch could captivate her as much as his was able to. Her body never felt like her own. It was as if he'd programmed her to respond to him and him alone.

"Are you trying to wash me away?" Tiny asked, startling her.

Jerking at his sudden presence, she slipped on the cold tile and almost tumbled through the glass door. Tiny caught her around the waist bringing her up against his body. The easy way he held her startled her. His arms banded around her protecting her from harm.

"Be careful. I'm not in the mood to visit the hospital with you again. You've been there far too much."

He released her and spun her around to face him.

"I only wanted a shower, and you should wear a fucking bell or something. Don't you know not to creep up on someone, let alone a woman?"

Tiny shrugged. "I told you tonight was mine. I've already wasted an hour with work when I promised you my attention." He gripped her hair, wrapping the length around his fist.

Tilting her head back, Eva had no choice but to follow his lead. He pulled on the length then turned her back to the spray.

"Have you ever been fucked in the shower?" he asked.

She kept her eyes closed to stop herself from getting water in them. "Yes," she said.

He tensed behind her. "Who with?" He growled the question at her.

"Someone you will never know."

"You're lying." Tiny turned her back to face him.

"No, I'm not lying. I wasn't a virgin when you

took me. I've had a lot of sex before I met you. I just don't advertise what I've done."

"You've not been fucked in the ass."

Her cheeks warmed. "I know."

"Who fucked you in the shower?" Tiny asked.

Was he jealous, or was she seeing things?

"I'm not telling you." He wouldn't let her go. Reaching behind her, she covered his hands with her own. "Let me go."

"No, I want to know who touched you."

"You've been married, Tiny. You've fucked enough women to last you a lifetime. I know. I've seen you in action." Glaring up at him, Eva would not back down.

"I don't like it."

Tiny didn't need to know she'd only been with one man before him. Her past would stay there.

"You'll have to deal with it," Eva said. "I'm not a virgin. I gave that up a long time ago."

"Fine." He let her hair go and pushed on her shoulders. She went down on her knees before him. "Tonight you're still mine, and I'll make sure you can't remember the last time you were in the shower with him."

She watched him fist his cock before ordering her to open her lips. Eva took him into her mouth and showed him how hot it could be to fuck in the shower.

****

Kelsey stared at the big man sat in her front room. Killer kept coming back, and she didn't know how she was supposed to keep him away. He scared her. The whole of The Skulls scared her. When he told her everything that happened between Nash and Sophia she'd been terrified. Being with Killer meant risking a lot of pain.

Angel had lost a baby because of the pain of their enemies. The last time she visited the club she overheard some of the men talking about Killer. His name was apt for what he could do.

She tensed as he stood up from his seat and started looking through her books. His hands were large.

"The Lions thought it was funny to watch him kill whoever they told him to."

"I heard he could snap a neck like Lash with his bare hands."

Biting her lip, she turned away to gather her wits about her. He'd stayed with her, and she'd slept in his room at The Skulls' compound. They hadn't gotten naked or had sex, but those hands that had taken a life had also given her pleasure. A lot of pleasure. Her cheeks heated recalling the feel of his fingers stroking between her thighs.

"What's going on, Kels?" Killer asked.

She jumped. Her hand went to her chest to feel her thumping heart. "You scared me!"

"Sorry, you've been avoiding me. What's going on? You're acting like I'm going to hurt you."

His arms were folded over his chest.

Great work, Kelsey. He's defensive.

"Nothing is the matter." She poured out the hot water into their cups to make them both a cup of tea. Kelsey preferred tea to coffee. Tate hated the scent of coffee. She loved her friend and wouldn't dream of hurting her.

She noticed her hand was shaking. Putting the kettle down, she tensed as he grabbed her hand. He moved so quickly around her kitchen. "You're shaking."

"Sorry," she said.

He frowned. "There was a time you melted against me, Kels. You look petrified."

"I'm tired."

Slowly, he turned her around and pushed her up against the fridge.

"Really?" Killer leaned down. His hands went around her neck, his thumbs pushing her chin up.

Her heart raced.

"The Lions thought it was funny to watch him kill whoever they told him to."

"I heard he could snap a neck like Lash with his bare hands."

The conversation she overheard replayed again in her mind. She panicked at the thought of those hands cutting off the air she breathed.

Bringing her hands up she shoved him away quickly. "No, stop!" She yelled the words at the same time her hands went around her neck.

"What the fuck? I was going to kiss you. It has been too damn long since I felt your lips on mine." He yelled right back at her, not backing down.

"I heard some men talking. I know what you're capable of and what you used to do for The Lions. The people you killed for fun, the women." Everything came pouring out, and she couldn't stop it.

Killer paled. She saw his change of color and the horror on his face.

"You think I'd kill you?" he asked, standing tall. He looked wounded. Her words had hit him hard.

"I don't know." She felt like an idiot. Killer had never hurt her. Every time he touched her, he did it with care.

"I would never hurt you, Kels. Fuck." He slammed his fist against the wall.

She winced, knowing it had to hurt.

"Who did you hear talking about me?" he asked, stepping close.

"I don't know. "

"You know the fucking Skulls. Tell me who you heard and tell me now."

Licking her lips, she felt her hands shaking. Kelsey wanted to take everything back she'd said. The anger in his eyes scared her, but it wasn't directed at her.

"It was Butch and Zero."

The two men were known gossipers.

"Good. I'll send someone else to pick you on Friday for the party." He turned away to leave.

"No, Killer, wait."

She charged after him, not wanting him to leave for fear of what would happen to him.

He stopped at the door with his back to her.

"Please don't leave. I'm sorry. I'm an idiot. Please, come back."

"No. I've got shit to do. I shouldn't have come here. It was a mistake."

Killer left, taking his anger with him. The door slammed making her tense.

Running to her phone, she quickly dialed Tate's number.

"Hello." Murphy answered the phone.

"I need to speak to Tate. It's an emergency."

Whatever Killer had to do, it wasn't going to go well for some of the men.

Chapter Five

Tiny woke up hearing his cell phone ringing. The sun was shining in the partially opened curtains. His cell phone stopped ringing. Rubbing a hand down his face to clear the sleep from his mind, he glanced down to see Eva asleep on his chest. He kept one hand on her back as he reached out to the cabinet beside the bed.

Tate's name flashed on the screen. He was about to dial her number again when his cell phone went off. Clicking the accept button, he put the phone to his ear.

"What could you possibly need this early in the morning?" Tiny asked.

Eva moaned and started to wake up.

"Is that Eva? You've got Eva in your bed? Is she there willingly?"

His daughter was going to spoil his good mood. "Of course she bloody is here willingly. What kind of man do you take me for?"

"I got my answer. I know you, Dad. Piss you off and you give me what I want." She giggled, which only riled him up more.

"Tell her to stop being mean," Eva said, mumbling.

He relayed her words. Tate grew quiet, changing the conversation. "I phoned up because Kelsey is worried. Killer was with her last night, and to cut a rather long story short, he's after Zero and Butch."

Eva moved off him, and Tiny stood staring out of the window.

"What do you mean?"

"He's called Killer for a reason. Something tells me Butch and Zero are not going to last much longer if he gets hold of them. They've pissed him off. Murphy is trying to find him, and I'm on my way to the club. He didn't go back to the compound last night."

Tiny heard his daughter on the move.

"Fine, I'll be at the club. He should listen to me."

Eva snorted and climbed out of bed. He stared down the line of her back. Bruises from his fingers decorated her hips. His cock swelled at the sight of her walking away.

"I'd hurry up unless you want to burry some of your men." Tate hung up.

"Trouble in paradise?" Eva asked.

"Someone has pissed off Killer. I've got to go."

"Okay."

"Are you coming with me?" He checked through the drawers and wardrobe finding them empty.

"Your room is next door, and yes, I'll come with you. I've got some jobs to sort out with Tate. It'll be fun to see who can beat Killer."

Leaving the room he quickly grabbed a shirt and jeans before heading downstairs. Eva was already stood by the door. She wore a pair of jeans and a shirt. He was struck by how young she looked. Last night he'd not given a thought to her age.

"Don't go all coy on me now," she said.

He ignored her, grabbing his keys and unlocking the door. Eva followed him out the door. Handing her a helmet, he quickly put one on himself and climbed on his bike. She moved behind him, holding onto his waist as he started up his machine.

Her arms felt good, and he was struck by the memory of her on her knees in the shower. He'd backed her up to the corner of the stall and fucked her mouth, going as deep as he could go. Tiny hadn't found release in her mouth but pulled her to her feet and forced her up the wall. He'd fucked her hard against the wall. Their bodies had slapped together with hot water cascading down around them. He shook the image from his thoughts.

His cock thickened even as he tried to concentrate on riding. She tightened her hands around his waist, and he kept his focus on the road.

Thirty minutes later he arrived at the compound. Some of the prospects were already working on the cars at the front of the building. He ran a garage along with many other businesses. They needed to keep their bikes in working order, and having a garage allowed him to take care of his boys and the bikes. It also meant people didn't look too closely at his investments.

Parking his bike, Eva climbed off, handing him the helmet. She flicked her head forward and shook out her hair. "There's nothing like helmet hair," she said, turning on her heel and walking away.

He couldn't believe how much of a challenge she was turning out to be. Tiny knew she wasn't staying beyond Friday even though he wanted her to. So many women stayed around to ask their men what they should do or waited for them to give instructions. Eva was independent, and nothing was ever going to change that about her. She didn't need him to tell her what to do, but she gave him the control in the bedroom. He was starting to believe that Eva was only collecting memories to take away with her, and it hurt him more than he liked to think about.

Putting both of their helmets on the bike he followed her inside to where the commotion was taking place. He saw a bottle being thrown across the room and smash against the wall. Lash and Angel were stood together, shaking their heads. Tate was watching the fighting.

His daughter turned around to look at him. "You were a little late. Killer got here about five minutes ago."

Pushing his way through the crowd, Tiny saw Killer still wore his Skulls cut.

"He's in a really bad mood. I wouldn't recommend getting involved," Tate said.

Murphy stood next to Tate, guarding her.

"What the fuck is this over?" Tiny asked, getting annoyed. Two of his tables were broken with multiple chairs shattered around the room. Zero and Butch were stood at opposite ends with Killer in the middle.

"What the fuck, man? What did we do to you?" Butch asked.

Zero had blood coming down from his nose, and bruising had already started to come around his left eye. Tiny knew it was going to sting when the adrenaline wore off.

"Kelsey heard these two talking smack about Killer. He's pissed about them talking about his past and is taking retribution," Tate said. "She's on her way. I asked her to come in case you couldn't talk the giant down."

"Giant?" Tiny asked, wincing as Killer kicked out at Butch, hitting the other man in the stomach. Butch went down quickly. Killer picked Butch up and threw him against the wall.

"Tate nicknamed Killer 'Giant'," Murphy said, smiling.

"Yeah, he's like a giant, look. Killer lifted Butch up as if he was rag doll. He's tall and in control. He's a giant. I wish I had some popcorn." She rubbed her stomach.

Zero charged at Killer and jumped on the other man's back. His arm went around Killer's neck. "Back down!"

Tiny watched the struggle. This fight was between brothers. He would only interfere if someone lashed out wrongly or made the fight dirty.

"No, you should learn to keep your fucking mouths shut." Killer leaned forward, flinging Zero off his back to the floor.

Zero blocked a punch and spun away from the kick intended for his ribs.

Tiny would give Killer credit. The bastard was determined to win.

Butch finally got up off the floor. He looked a little dazed and threw a beer can at Killer. "I'm here."

Killer turned, intent on causing destruction to the other brother. Tiny tensed, waiting for his moment to intervene.

"Killer, stop!" The feminine voice interrupted all the action. Kelsey charged through the crowd. At her voice Killer did stop.

"Yeah, stop this shit," Butch said, pissing the other man off. Killer started walking toward Butch again. Pain was clearly his intention.

Kelsey ran in front of Butch putting her hand up. "I said stop."

Killer stopped, staring at her.

"Your woman is going to protect me," Butch said, smirking. Bruises were all over Butch's face from being treated like a doll. Tiny would have recommended the other man be silent.

"Shut the fuck up. He'll hurt you and make you wish you were dead." Kelsey had her hand up. She took a step forward until that hand was pressed to Killer's chest.

Tiny watched Killer's jaw tense as he stared at the woman in front of him.

"I should have known it would take a cherry blonde to tame him," Tate said. "I touched her hair up a week ago."

Zero and Butch stood together behind Kelsey,

who stared at Killer without flinching.

"Move out of the way, Kels."

"It was my fault. You do not need to take your anger out on them. They're not the problem. I shouldn't have been listening into their conversation. Stop this. It's not worth it."

Killer wiped at his mouth where a small mark of blood was in the corner.

"This wasn't about what they fucking said. It was the fact they were talking about me." Killer slapped his chest. "What I did for my past club is no one's fucking business but mine." He turned to glare at Murphy. "You told me my past would fucking stay there."

The pain in Killer's eyes hurt Tiny. He felt responsible for all of his boys' pain. The man before him was hurting and hurting bad.

Before he could say anything, Killer turned back to Kelsey.

"I killed people for my club. I did what I had to in order to fucking survive. I killed men and women. They gave the order, and they were dead. It was in my past, and if I had to kill anyone to protect you, I would." Killer took a step forward, gripping Kelsey's arms.

Tate tensed, clearly ready to kick some giant ass if Kelsey was harmed. Tiny would hold her back. There was no way he'd let his daughter get hurt if she started. The way Murphy moved in front of her, the other man was of the same mind.

"I won't apologize for who I was. This is the man I am, and I'm capable of killing anyone, and if I was asked to protect you or this club then the bastards would die." Killer slammed his lips down on Kelsey. She didn't fight him.

When it was over, Killer released her and walked out of the club. Silence fell over the club. Butch stumbled into one of the sweet-butt's arms. Sophia rushed to Zero's side, checking to make sure nothing was broken. Zero had been close to Sophia, and it showed.

Tiny glared as Zero smiled. The way Zero touched Sophia left no one in doubt of the man's feelings for Nash's woman. Tiny had warned Zero about poaching. Tiny hoped he didn't have to kick the guy's ass to make him back down. Tate went to Kelsey. Eva moved to stand beside him. "You need to deal with Zero. His feelings could get the whole club killed."

"I know."

She took his hand, offering him her strength.

"I've kicked enough of my boys' asses."

"If it needs to be done then you've got no choice but to do it." Eva squeezed his hand then stepped away.

"Come back to my office," he said, wanting inside her tight warmth more than he wanted to deal with club business.

"Can't. The night is over, and we're back to normal." She went on her toes and kissed his cheek. "Business comes first, and you'd agree with me."

She turned away completely, moving away from him.

He watched her until she disappeared completely from his sight. When she was gone he grabbed, Lash, Nash, and Murphy before heading out to 'round the back of the compound for some privacy.

"What's this about?" Lash asked.

Lighting up a cigarette, Tiny took a deep drag, feeling relaxed for a few short seconds. "Your women go into town regularly, right?"

Turning to the men, he saw the confusion on their faces.

"I've not asked. Tate does go to the salon. Since being run over she doesn't go into town alone. I'm with her. I've not seen anything strange," Murphy said.

"Same here."

"Sophia and I have been dealing with the house. It still needs a lot of work. What's going on here?" Nash asked.

"Something doesn't sit right with me from your kidnapping." Tiny pointed at Nash. "We've talked about it, and you said they worked for someone else. What did they say?" They had been over the same ground a thousand times. No matter what Nash said, Tiny couldn't piece together what was bothering him.

"Gill was terrified. All of the men were scared. They were hired by men that were clearly serious. It has got to take something to make a bunch of thugs scared, right?" Nash asked.

"What are you thinking, boss?" Lash asked.

"The Lions have been handled, and the drugs Alex sorted out. I think there's another threat out there. I don't know. Something doesn't feel right." Taking another deep drag on his cigarette, Tiny looked over the landscape. Fort Will was his town. It was where he'd lived his whole life. He'd brought the town out of the gutter, giving it protection and striving to make a living.

"We'll keep an eye out and see if anyone looks out of the ordinary," Nash said.

"Okay." He dismissed them. They were all leaving when he called Murphy back. "Get me Whizz. I need to speak to him."

****

After Killer tried to hurt Zero and Butch, nothing else happened. When Friday arrived, Eva was more than ready to finish the party and get home. Her father had landed at the airport a few hours ago, and he was on his way to the house. Tiny was locked in his office. Their one night together hadn't changed anything between them.

Staring at her reflection Eva nodded. She couldn't change her dress or rush to the hairdressers to fix her hair. Running her hands down her thighs she waited for her nerves to stop. She was nervous about her father. Ned Walker had the ability to spot something within a person that they wanted no one else to see.

The last thing she needed was for her father to be angry at Tiny. They'd slept together. She didn't need her father defending her honor or anything stupid like that.

Picking up her two light suitcases she headed downstairs and placed them beside the door. Tiny's door was still shut. He'd been locked in the office all night. She'd phoned Alex to tell him in case Tiny wasn't asking for help. Twice she walked upstairs coming down with heavier cases each time. She was surprised by how much she owned.

On the final trip Tiny was stood at the bottom of the stairs. He wore a pair of new jeans and white shirt. It was the best anyone was going to get for him to be smart. He rarely wore a suit.

She felt her pussy clench at the sight of him. His age never affected her. The man himself though, affected her deeply. She knew what it felt like to have him pounding inside her. Every part of him was strong.

Licking her lips, she held onto the case.

"You're still leaving?"

"I'm not needed here anymore. It's time I moved on. I'm not getting any younger," she said, trying to make a joke.

"Is that supposed to be directed at me?" he asked. He folded his arms over his chest. Once again she remembered him holding her in place in the shower. Fuck, he truly had wiped the memory of every other previous lover, even though there *was* only one. She couldn't even think of shower sex without thinking of him.

"No. I've never had a problem with your age." Tucking her hair behind her ear, she stared past his shoulder. "I told you I was going. I never led you to believe I was staying. Tate is pregnant. She's going to be a mother herself. You've got the club. I need to find something for me."

She stopped talking as his fingers caressed over her knee. Up he went to her thigh caressing and stroking her.

"You've got me."

She expelled her breath and stared into his eyes. "It's not enough."

"Goddamn it, Eva. What do I need to do?" he asked.

"Nothing." The door was banged invading their time together. "That's my dad."

Tiny didn't move away from the stairs stopping her from answering the door. "I thought he was supposed to meet us at the compound."

"He rented a car. He's taking me to the airport straight from the club. Tate organized the baby shower so I was around to see all three of them." His fingers were still caressing her thigh.

Another bang on the door made her jump. Ned wouldn't wait for long before he made his impatience known.

"She's going to need your help. I can pay you double to stay."

"No." She pushed his hand away. "I'm going, Tiny."

He moved out of the way, not that she gave him a choice. Going to the door, she opened it without looking. Ned, her father, stood with his arms folded. He was as large as Tiny. He was older than Tiny, but he kept himself in good shape.

"Daddy," she said, going into his arms.

"Baby girl, I was beginning to worry I'd forgotten our arrangements." He embraced her, squeezing her close.

"I was getting the last of my bags. Sorry it took me so long to open the door." She pulled away, smiling at him.

Even as she smiled, happy to see her father, a part of her was hurting at leaving Tiny behind.

"Let's get these bags in the car, and then I really need a drink."

"Did you come alone?" she asked, needing him to talk to avoid the obvious question.

"Yeah, Gavin is training my fighters. He's looking forward to seeing you again."

She tensed at the other man's name. "Dad, I'm not going back to him. Any matchmaking you've got planned can stop today."

"I'm not going to do anything, honey. Gavin's a real asset to me." Ned took the cases from her. Together they walked to the car. Tiny had disappeared into his office. She hoped he hadn't seen her reaction to Gavin's name.

At the car, she handed over her cases.

"What's gone on between you and Tiny?" Ned asked.

"Nothing." She wouldn't meet his eyes.

"You've fucked him, haven't you?"

She must look like a strawberry. Her cheeks had to be on fire. Ned always got to the point with everything. She'd grown up around a lot of gruff language.

"I don't want to talk about it." She made to walk

away. He caught her wrist stopping her from escaping.

"If you want to stay I'll be happy to spend a few hours with you and leave you here."

She looked up at him seeing the sincerity in his eyes.

"I'm leaving. I've got to leave. Tiny hasn't done anything wrong. This is entirely my decision. Please don't start thinking he's done something wrong. He hasn't."

"Who are you trying to convince?" Ned asked, folding his arms. She stared at the tattoos across his knuckles. The words "FUCK OFF" stared at her. He'd gotten them in prison many years ago.

"No one. I'm just convincing you so you won't kick his ass." She smiled at him, hoping he wouldn't see past the lie.

"Honey, I'll be kicking his ass for letting you go."

Shaking her head, she watched him place each case in the trunk of the car. "You won't."

Ned slammed the trunk down. His gaze went to the house. Looking behind her, she wondered what he was looking at. The doorway was bare.

"Your man is looking at you through the window. He's not going to beg you, Eva. If this is what you want, then you're going to be disappointed."

Letting out a sigh, she turned away from the house.

"I'm not, Dad. Leave it alone." She tucked some hair behind her ear and started walking toward the house.

"Eva." Ned called her name. Turning back to look at him, she waited for him to respond. "What arc you running from?"

Staring at her father, the man who'd been the saint in her story but the devil in so many others, she wondered how he could be two different people. She'd never once asked about her mother or why he did what he did.

Eva knew why she was leaving, but she knew her father would make her face what she was running from. She was running from pain. Tiny was her one weakness, and she'd been brought up to never have a weakness and to face the person causing her pain.

"Your feelings for him are not going to change, not even if you put another state between you," Ned said.

"Is that how you felt with my mother?" she asked. She saw him tense, but she didn't care. Tiny was her weakness as he was the only man, besides her father, who could cause her pain.

Spinning on her heel she walked back into the house. Tiny was stood in the doorway of his office. "You're really going?"

"Yes."

He stared into her eyes. She saw the lust, the fire, and the burning passion smoldering within his depths.

What was she waiting for? Eva knew he wouldn't beg her to stay with him.

"Sorry," he said. Tiny hadn't broken eye contact with her.

"What? Why?"

"I'm sorry for the pain I've caused you." He stood hard, unyielding against the door. "The women were a distraction. I never meant to hurt you. It has been too long since I cared about anyone. Tate is my daughter and I loved her, but being with other women would never hurt her."

"Where is all of this coming from?" she asked.

Tiny stepped forward, cupping her cheek. She felt the calluses on his palm as he caressed her flesh. "You're leaving, and I need you to know."

She pressed her hand on top of his. "The leader of

The Skulls is apologizing to me?"

"You deserve it. All the shit I put you through, it's the least I can do."

Eva frowned at him. "You've been talking to Tate."

His daughter was the only person to make Tiny see reason.

"She has a way about her that is hard to ignore."

Kissing his palm, she stepped away. "I'm going to the club. I'll see you there."

Without looking back she grabbed her purse and walked out to the car where her father was waiting.

Her heart was pounding, and she hated the pain she was feeling at walking away. Her love for Tiny wouldn't go away overnight, but she wasn't ready for this, and neither was he.

"Let's get this over with," she said, climbing into the car.

Ned didn't say anything as he started up the car. Staring at the wing mirror she saw Tiny walk out of the house. Staring straight ahead, she wouldn't let herself give into the need to go back to him. He was her past, and she'd learned long ago it was easier to walk away than stay fighting a lost cause.

****

Snitch walked through town wearing the garb of a trucker. He'd killed the man who owned the milk truck outside of town at a motel. No one paid him any attention as he blended in. His hair fell around his face, covering up the tattoo on his neck. Keeping his hands hooked into the straps down his body, he stared left and right, taking everything in. For twenty years he'd been waiting for the right time to come back and claim what was his. When he'd been pushed out of his town, he'd lost everything. Snitch didn't have a club or anyone he could trust.

Everyone he knew had died that night. Over the years he'd planned and built up a club going from state to state to find the men who'd follow him without question. Building up a club was not fucking easy, especially, a club he that needed to have his back and be willing to take a bullet for him.

Looking around the town, he breathed in the fresh air knowing his twenty years of work were about to pay off. He'd never acted rashly. The years he'd waited were worth it as he felt victory so close at hand.

Tiny sure had turned the town into a profitable area.

His men were waiting for him over thirty miles out of town. Snitch had wanted to be the one to check out his old home. Each of his men had explored the town of Fort Wills without being detected, and it was his turn to check out his old home. The people were so cheery. None of them knew what he had planned for this little town. The law enforcement would go after The Skulls. He had a plan, and it was all down to timing. During his years he'd learned to become a patient man to go after what he wanted. The men had been with him for some time. They were much better than the crew that had died over twenty years ago.

"Murphy, we've got to go," Tate said. "How can I have a baby shower without being there?"

He rounded the corner to see Tiny's daughter stood with her hands on her hips. Next to her was a Skull. The leather cut of his jacket showcased who he belonged to. Slowing his pace, Snitch saw the Skull putting a wicker basket into the back of the truck.

"Hold your fucking horses, woman. You've turned the club into a fucking fairy land. I'm not having you bitch at me over missing something," Murphy said, opening the basket to show his woman. Snitch didn't see what it was. He didn't need to. The glow coming from Tate was evidence of what he'd done.

"Oh, baby. Have I told you how much I love you?"

Tate threw herself at Murphy.

Pulling out his cell phone, Snitch looked down at the screen, heading straight for the couple. When he was close he made sure they'd have to see him. Some thrill at being seen went up Snitch's spine. The little shit wouldn't know him. None of Tiny's club would know him. He'd heard about Mikey being killed, which was a fucking shame. Snitch would have liked to have killed the fucker himself for turning against him.

Dropping his cell phone under the man's truck, Snitch put his hands up in the air. "I'm so sorry, man. I wasn't looking where I was going. My woman was on the phone, complainin'. You know how it is?" It took every ounce of willpower not to laugh. Snitch saw Murphy glare at him, bending down to grab the cell phone.

"Get the fuck out and watch where you're going next time."

Yeah, he was going, and when he came back, the bastard and the women were going to be dead.

Chapter Six

Sipping at his beer Tiny watched Ned from the corner of his compound. Tate was soaking up the attention, and Eva was stood with his daughter. The two women were the best of friends. No one would even suspect that Eva helped to raise his daughter. He was sure if it wasn't for Eva, his daughter would have been impossible to tame.

Whizz approached him. The smile on the other man's face wouldn't alert any of the club to the possible danger they could be in.

"Hi, boss," Whizz said, taking a gulp of his drink.

"What do you have for me?" Tiny asked.

"Nothing."

Frowning, he turned to the other man at his side. Whizz had once been a Lion, one of his enemies. When The Lions went down, Murphy brought three men to him who he felt would be a benefit to his own club. Whizz, Time, and Killer were brilliant, and Tiny knew the men were loyal.

"What do you mean you've got nothing?" Snitch was not the kind of man to *not* have a record.

"Exactly what I mean, which is fucking messed up. No one can get around without being noticed. This man you asked me to look into pretty much disappeared after you took over Fort Wills. All the dates you've given me actually add up." Whizz took another long pull on his beer. "You know what it means?"

"Yeah, he's off the grid, and there's no way for us to know where he is."

"He can't be found unless he wants to be. If this man is a danger to us and Fort Wills then you're going to need to alert the others. I can't find him, and if I can't find him, I can't prepare us for it." Whizz was looking around the club.

"This could be down to my own paranoia," Tiny said. Over the last year he'd been hit left, right, and fucking center. Was it making him think of a dead man as an enemy? There was a reason for someone to go off the grid, and that's because they're fucking dead.

"I looked at this man's file, Tiny. Fort Wills didn't stop him as they were fucking terrified, but the guy has a record from before then." Whizz turned away from the group. "He doesn't give a fuck about anyone. He doesn't have a code or care who he hits. Women, children, the innocent, he kills them all, and those who take his fancy, he tortures them."

Tiny didn't need to be reminded. The image of the girl's pain flashed across his mind. He knew the kind of pain Snitch could inflict, and it wasn't good.

"Good work," Tiny said, slapping the man on the back. He was no closer to knowing if Snitch was alive.

"I'm sorry I can't give you any good news."

"Don't worry about it. Enjoy the party." Tiny felt it was going to be the last party for a long time.

Leaving his alcove he joined in with the celebration. Angel, Sophia, and Tate were all glowing with happiness. He watched each of them preen under the attention. Murphy, Lash, and Nash didn't leave their sides. The pride in their expressions made Tiny chuckle.

"They remind me of you," Alex said, coming forward.

"Oh yeah, how?" Tiny asked, smiling at his brother-in-law.

Alex had become a friend Tiny never expected to have.

"When Patricia told you she was pregnant with Tate, you practically glowed. It was hard not to knock you the fuck out for knocking my sister up."

Tiny laughed, remembering the joy at the good news. Staring at his daughter, Tiny was proud of her. She was a fighter, and he knew she wouldn't take any shit from Murphy. Any of the sweet-butts who tried it on with her man got to feel Tate's wrath. She'd gotten his temper, which he didn't mind. He knew Murphy wouldn't get the chance to hurt her.

Eva's laughter caught her attention. Her head was thrown back, and the happiness in her eyes caught at his heart.

She's leaving.

"I heard about Eva," Alex said.

"What about her?"

"She's going back to Vegas with her father."

Tiny didn't say anything. There was no need seeing as there was nothing he could do to keep her home. Tate had phoned him earlier giving him a stern talking to. Nothing he said or did would ever bring Eva to him. She was untouchable. There was no point in him asking.

For many years he thought she was this sweet, innocent woman who couldn't handle the lifestyle. In many ways she reminded him a little of Patricia. Then, she'd turned the tables on him. She was probably more prepared for this lifestyle than his daughter. Tate had grown up with him being the head of The Skulls, and Eva had grown up with her father being the head of an underground fighting ring. The only difference between the two was he'd kept Tate as far from the club as he could whereas Ned welcomed his daughter with open arms.

Eva was a tough woman who was used to making hard decisions.

"You're not going to say anything to make her stay?" Alex asked.

"I'm not going to beg a woman, Alex. She's going, and it's for the best. This is not the place for her."

They were silent as both of them stared at the women in question.

"You're probably right. I doubt she'll be back. I heard Gavin is anxious to have her back," Alex said.

Before Alex had moved back to Fort Wills, the other man had lived in Vegas. Tiny knew Alex and Ned were friends, or at the very least business associates.

"Who's Gavin?"

Alex smirked, and Tiny just wanted to knock the smile off his face.

"Gavin is Eva's ex and also one of Ned's fighters."

Before he could ask any more questions, Alex moved away, finally leaving him alone. He wasn't an idiot. Alex had told him the truth about Eva on purpose. She hadn't been a virgin, but Tiny couldn't stop the feeling of jealousy consuming him.

Next Ned walked toward him. Staying still, Tiny waited for the other man to start a conversation. He understood any anger Ned felt as he knew the feeling when it came to Tate.

"You're going to let my daughter go?" Ned asked.

Tiny stared at Eva. She was so beautiful inside and out. He'd lost so much time where he could have called her his own.

"Yes."

He'd lost time and caused her heartache and pain.

"Eva won't be back. She won't be waiting for you. I'll make sure she has no choice but to move on," Ned said.

"Are you threatening me?" Tiny asked.

"No. I'm not going to kill you. What I'm going to

do is make sure my daughter is not standing around waiting for you. She deserves better than what you can give her."

"You're not going to kick my ass?" Tiny was surprised. He figured the other man would want to hurt him and make sure he couldn't father any more children.

"I'm on your turf, Tiny. I'm not some young person who doesn't know how to respect their boundaries. Come to Vegas and we'll see what happens."

Tiny respected the man more.

"My daughter is in love with you," Ned said. "I've seen her love before but never like this."

"I hurt her. She deserves so much more than me."

"And yet you've not taken your eyes off her." Ned nodded toward everyone else. "They all respect her and treat her like your old lady."

"Anyone who hurts or disrespects her answers to me."

"I heard a rumor that not long ago one of your men almost killed her by being fucking high. It was an accident or so I heard," Ned said.

Glancing at Nash, Tiny grit his teeth together. Nash had been under the influence of alcohol and drugs. The intoxicating substances didn't excuse his behavior, but Nash had worked like hell to get back on the straight and narrow.

"What about it?" Tiny asked.

"You beat the kid to a bloody pulp. Eva didn't even have a scratch on her, and you fought for her."

"What are you trying to say?" Tiny faced him.

"If you're going to hurt my daughter you would have done it. When was the last time you took another woman since your last time in Vegas?"

Tiny didn't answer him. He glared, waiting for him to make a point. Since their time in Vegas, Tiny hadn't been able to touch another woman. Stepping over the line with Eva had sealed his fate. No other woman would do for him. Even though Vegas hadn't been that long ago, Tiny felt a difference in himself.

"I see you're going to be a hard ass. Your loss. Evangeline is a tough woman. I made sure she could handle herself."

He noticed Ned said her whole name. Tiny loved her name. It was beautiful like the woman.

"We'll be out of your way within the hour."

Ned moved away without a word. Tiny watched him go seeing the arrogance and confidence in his movement.

There was nothing he could do to stop her. Leaving the party behind, he went to his office. He didn't shut the door as he didn't want any of his men to be getting the wrong idea.

"You're hiding away in here?" Eva asked.

She was stood leaning against the doorframe.

"I'm not hiding. I'm waiting." He sipped at his beer, staring down the length of her body. Memories of the last time he'd seen her in this room ran through his mind. Her body had been naked, open and waiting for him.

"Tate's excited about everything." Eva didn't move from her spot.

Tiny caressed the spot on the desk where he'd tasted and taken her.

"I'll always remember what you looked like when you took my cock."

He heard her gasp. Glancing up, he saw her advance into the room. She rounded the desk, wrapped her arms around his neck and brought him down to her.

She claimed his lips, plunging her tongue into his mouth. He gripped her ass, pressing his hard dick against her stomach. Their moans mingled together, and with his other hand, he held her head still.

His heart was pounding, and the need was intense. Never once had he ever felt this way with anyone, not even Patricia. He felt like he was drowning in her essence.

"Don't go," he said, whispering the words against her lips.

"I've got to." She broke the kiss, leaning her head against his chest.

"No, you don't. I'll take care of you."

She stroked his chest, running her fingers across his patch.

"No." Eva pulled out of his arms. Her lips were bruised from his kisses. "You'll forget about me soon enough." She caressed his cheek then moved away. He followed her out and paused as Tate pulled her into a hug.

His men offered their wishes and goodbyes. Ned led the way outside, and he went with the crowd. She waved to everyone climbing in the car. He broke through the crowd, watching Ned pull away from the curb.

Eva turned around and stared at him. Her hand was up, waving to him.

Tiny couldn't tear his gaze away as she drove out of his life.

****

"Eva?" Ned asked.

She was staring at Tiny, who stood with his hands fisted at his sides. There was nothing for her to do. She had to get away. If she gave into him then he'd regret his decision. Tiny was not ready for any kind of commitment. Living with him had made her aware of the kind of man he was.

"Don't, Dad." She spoke still seeing the man she

loved getting smaller as they moved away.

When she could no longer see Tiny's outline she turned back around to stare out of the front of the car. The scenery didn't catch her eye. She was too busy remembering the feel of Tiny's lips on hers. They were silent for several minutes. Eva kept her gaze out of the window watching Fort Wills leave her behind.

"Gavin is looking forward to you coming home," Ned said, starting a conversation.

Turning to him, she glared. "Don't go there. Nothing is going to happen between Gavin and me."

"He's sorry over what happened. It's time for you both to move on."

"When I move on it will not be with Gavin or any of your men." She grabbed her sunglasses from her bag.

Eva frowned. She'd never once told her father the reason why she'd moved on. "How do you know what happened between him and me?"

"Gavin told me. You're not the kind of woman to just leave without a reason. I know you left me a note, but it's still out of character for you." Ned maneuvered around a large milk truck. "He was embarrassed by what happened."

"What did you do?" she asked.

"Your relationship is your own business. I didn't hurt him over what went down between you. However, the slut he was with is gone, and he got six months rotation without pay."

"Is that all?"

"I may have taken him into the ring and kicked his ass for sending my daughter away." Ned didn't take his eyes off the road.

"I'm surprised he's still living." She flipped open her phone to see a sad face on the screen from Tate. Smiling, she deleted the message and put her phone back away.

"He makes a lot of money, and men fuck up. Gavin was young, and he made a mistake."

"Gavin fucked up, and I'm not going to hold anything against him. I won't be having anything to do with him." She sat back against the chair letting her thoughts drift to the man she left behind. The women he'd been with had hurt her, but she never actually caught him in the act. They'd never meant anything to each other either, so it wasn't like he was cheating on her.

"Tiny is a good man, but he's got the same problems that Gavin has. He can't keep it in his pants."

She slammed her hand on the dash board. "No, you do not get to do that. Tiny is none of your business. He never will be, and I won't be discussing him with you now or in the future. Yes, I loved him, and I loved his daughter." Her hand hurt from slapping down on the hard surface. "I will not be dating or spending any time with Gavin. Do not think to throw us together. I'll work for you again, but I won't have anything to do with the men."

"If you love him, why are you leaving him?" Ned asked.

"Sometimes to help others you need to know when to back away. Tiny doesn't need me around, and we're not good for each other. Kind of like you and Mom."

She saw him tense out of the corner of her eye.

"Yeah, Gavin is such a good man. He told me what happened with my mother. I know you killed her." Eva couldn't believe she was speaking as if death was a natural topic of conversation.

"He shouldn't have said anything."

"It doesn't matter anymore. Nothing is going to

change what happened. She's gone." Eva had never gotten the chance to know her mother.

"I never told you anything about it or her."

Staying silent, Eva drummed her fingers on her leg. Her father was a dangerous man, yet she'd never been afraid of him, not even when she'd been naughty growing up. Even knowing how dangerous she was she didn't hate him. This was the world she'd grown up in. Ned wouldn't kill her, and he wouldn't kill Tiny. Both men were too important in their little world.

"She was a stripper I knocked up," Ned said.

Eva had seen pictures of her mother growing up. She'd been a beautiful, slender woman with blonde hair, but she hadn't been a loyal woman.

"Your mother wasn't known for being faithful. Many men had known the pleasure she could have."

Closing her eyes, she didn't know if she needed to hear any more.

"Why did you kill her?" Eva asked. She couldn't mourn a woman she never knew. What people remembered about her was not nice either.

"She put you in danger. You mother was an addict, and she was selling her body to whoever would give her what she wanted." Ned pulled up in the airport. He must have paid for a space as one was reserved near the door. "She took you to one of the men who serviced her habit and sold her out to men. I found you on the floor that was covered in needles, Eva. She'd taken you because no one would babysit. Your mother didn't give a fuck about you. She didn't even care that you could have been hurt. One of my men got you out while I ended the shit she would have put you through."

Tears filled her eyes at the horror he described. She couldn't even remember it, but how could she? She'd been young, a baby.

"I never told you about her because you were better than her." Ned turned the engine off. "Eva, I'm proud of you, and I hope you can forgive me for the hurt I've caused you."

She smiled even as the tears started to fall. "I'm not hurt by you, Dad. It's not your fault she didn't care. I love you." She wrapped her arms around him, tightly. He was the only person she'd ever been able to turn to.

"Good. We better get going before we miss our flight."

For the next hour Eva was too busy dealing with her suitcases and getting ready for her flight. Ned took care of everything else, and she noticed he was on the phone a lot.

After purchasing a book she took a seat in the waiting area where everyone was sat or walking around. Her cell phone went off as her father joined her.

Answering the call she saw it was Tate.

"Hello," she said.

"You're really going?"

Rubbing her temple, Eva ignored her father and listened to Tate.

"We've talked about this. It's time for me to go."

"Something is going on. You know that. Dad is acting even more quiet than usual. Since you've gone he's locked himself in his office." Tate sounded worried, and Eva hated hearing the other woman worried.

"Tate, everything is going to be fine." She didn't know what else to say to the younger woman.

"You don't know that. Please, come back."

Gritting her teeth, she glanced at her father. Ned raised his brow at her, waiting for her to argue back.

"No. Tate, I'll come and visit you, but my life is in Vegas. I've been away too long."

"We went to Vegas together. Your life is not

there."

"We've got to go, Eva," Ned said, pointing to the waiting queue.

"I'm sorry, Tate, I've got to go. Please, keep in touch." Before Tate could say anything else, she closed her phone, turned it off and followed her father toward their seat. She wasn't surprised to see them in first class. Eva never had a problem flying economy, but Ned always liked the best.

She strapped into her seat and took several deep breaths. Eva hated leaving Tate and Fort Wills. Tapping her fingers on her leg she listened to all the instructions for the start of flights.

"You're nervous," Ned said.

"No, I'm fine." She'd never had a problem with flying. Looking out of the window she tried to ignore the pain in her chest. Tiny and all the good memories she had of her time in the small town ran through her mind. When she'd left Gavin and her father she hadn't been looking for anything. Stumbling into Fort Wills and getting the job as Tate's nanny had been pure luck.

The plane took off, and she closed her eyes needing to relax. Her father lay back, holding her hand. She didn't say anything as the rest of her life was made up for her.

You're making the right decision. Keep moving forward.

She and Tiny hadn't been together, but his actions still hurt her. While he'd been fucking everything in sight, men had been told to stay away from her. She hadn't been asked on one date in all of her time at Fort Wills. The only time she spent in male company was with members of The Skulls. Vegas was her home, and she was going to move on no matter how bad it hurt.

****

Killer watched Kelsey hug a crying Tate. His boss was trapped in the office, and since Eva left the party had been kind of stilted. He slapped the bar ordering another beer. The prospect who served looked at him nervously.

"What?" Killer asked.

He didn't know the man's name and didn't care to find out.

"Nothing."

The prospect moved away as Zero took the seat beside him.

"I'm not in the mood for conversation," Killer said.

"I don't care. You threw me around the other day. The least you can do is have a beer with me." Zero reached forward grabbing a bottle of whiskey.

Sipping at his bottle, Killer did his best to keep his anger in check. He'd not spoken to Kelsey since the day she'd caught him hitting his brothers.

"You're not going to talk to me either?" Zero asked.

"No."

"Man, I'm sorry. We didn't even hear anyone listening to us."

"I don't give a fuck," Killer said, putting his empty bottle on the counter. "My past is my business. I don't give a fuck about anything else."

He got up ready to leave the compound. Walking past Kelsey and out of the pink fucking fairy castle, Killer took a deep breath of the fresh air. Heading toward his bike, he climbed on and turned the key in the ignition.

"Killer?" Kelsey's voice made him tense. Her voice was so sweet, and he loved hearing her talk. She was the first woman he loved to hear talk.

"What?" he asked, hating himself for the way he

spoke to her.

"You're not even going to look at me?"

Letting out a sigh, he turned his gaze onto her. She looked so fucking beautiful with her cherry blonde hair curled and hanging around her shoulders and down her back. He recalled stroking the length as they'd been making out. Killer had taken his time caressing her lips and waiting for her to open up to him.

"What do you want, Kels?" he asked, facing her.

"I'm sorry. I shouldn't have judged you for what I heard. I was wrong, and I'm sorry. I'm so sorry." She reached out, touching his hand.

He stared down at her pale fingers spread over his own fingers. Killer was older than Kelsey by five years. She had so much goodness within her even if she was a dental nurse. He hated dentists.

Taking hold of her fingers he brought her hand against his lips. She smelled like vanilla.

"Kels, everything they were talking about is true. I killed people with my bare hands. I did it for my club, and it's no excuse. If you can live with that then we can have a future, but I've got a feeling you don't want to live a life with me like that." He dropped her hand and straddled his bike. Killer wanted more than anything to pull her into his arms. She needed to know his past. He wasn't going to live in fear of her finding out.

"Killer, wait."

He didn't wait to hear what she had to say.

Chapter Seven

"I've got a driver waiting for us," Ned said.

Eva reached out grabbing her bag from the carousel going around. The rest of her luggage would be sent to her father's house on the outskirts of Vegas. "Good." She followed him outside to see Gavin stood against her father's car. Stopping, she stared at the man she left behind over eight years ago. The last time she saw him his ass had been thrusting away inside another woman. She'd stumbled on the scene and had left as quickly. Leaving her note for her father was one of her last correspondence with him.

"Is this why you were talking about him?" Eva asked, stopping to stare.

Gavin didn't have a patch on Tiny, at least not to her. Yes, he was tall and muscular like Tiny. Being a fighter, Gavin had no choice but to stay in top form. What Tiny had that Gavin lacked was maturity. Both men were covered in tattoos, but staring at Gavin she saw the teasing in his eyes.

Tiny didn't waste his time with teasing. There was an intensity with Tiny. He captured her attention and kept her caught within his web.

She started walking.

"Hello, Eva."

Staring at the man who'd sent her running, Eva nodded. "Gavin."

He opened the car door for her, and she climbed inside. Her father took the passenger scat as Gavin took behind the wheel.

"Did you have a good flight?"

Eva stayed silent. Ned looked back at her, and she raised a brow at him. There was no way she was going to be talking to Gavin if she didn't have to.

"Uneventful. Eva spent most of the journey reading a book."

Silence fell around them once again. Eva didn't try to talk. There was no need. Her father was trying to match-make.

After several minutes of no conversation Gavin and Ned started talking about work.

"Is the fight still on for tomorrow?" Ned asked.

"Yes. Lance is ready to prove himself. I'm thinking we can double our profit on this one fight," Gavin said.

She drowned them out, resting her head against the seat. The heat was intense, and she instantly missed the cooler air of Fort Wills. Thinking about Tiny made heat pulse between her thighs. She wanted him, and there was nothing she could do to stop her feelings for him.

Remembering Tiny, she quickly clicked her phone back on. The moment it loaded up, the cell phone buzzed.

Tiny: Did you get there?

Smiling, Eva remembered the first time Tate talked him into getting a cell phone. He broke five phones before Eva talked him through the process of texting.

Eva: I'm fine. Heading home to bed.

Several seconds passed, and she checked to see other texts from Tate. Lash and Nash had left her well wishes. All of them had become her family in the years she'd been with them. Christmases had been spent together, lunches, fairs and parties where they celebrated everything.

"Are you okay, honey?" Ned asked.

"Fine."

Tiny: I miss you.

There was nothing else she could say to that.

Biting her lip she pocketed her phone and waited for the journey to be over. Vegas was buzzing even during the day. It was summer, and many people were basking in the joy and gambling on display. Driving down the strip, Eva shook her head.

Tate was right. This was not her home, but she'd have to make a go of it. Thirty minutes later, Gavin pulled into the gym Ned owned where he trained his fighters. The law knew what Ned Walker did, but no one could connect anything to him.

Gavin opened the door for her. She ignored him going back into the gym she'd once called home.

"Ned, what the hell are you wearing?" One of the men stood to embrace her father. Eva didn't recognize him. His sheer size could put Killer to shame.

"I had a baby shower to get to. Lance, I'd like you to finally meet my daughter, Evangeline." Ned smiled at her. Stepping close she shook Lance's hand, making sure to be firm and hard as she did. Ned told her to make sure she didn't show weakness even in a handshake.

"It's nice to finally meet you," Lance said, glancing up and down at her dress.

She still wore the dress she'd picked for the baby shower.

Eva recognized many of the fighters working out around the gym, and she went to each of them to hug.

"Damn, girl, it has been too damn long since we had you around here keeping us in order," Frank said, kissing her cheek. They were like brothers to her. She'd grown up around them watching them advance into the lifestyle.

Ned Walker had his fingers in many baskets, but he never allowed his fighters to take the adventure of drugs or disease. If his men were with whores then they bagged their pole. She invested in condoms for the men to use.

Glancing to the counter she saw the condom bowl was empty.

"It's good to see you, Frank. How is everything going with you?" she asked.

He smiled, pulling his necklace from around his neck. "I got myself a wife. She's a good girl." Frank showed her the ring.

"Congratulations." She handed him the ring back.

She'd heard Erik and Mark were also fathers with women of their own. David was still a player.

"Right, boys. We've got some training to do, and my girl needs to acquaint herself with the books. She'll be working around here, and I expect respect for her." Ned showed her to the back of the office. He told her the codes to the safe, pulling out the books for her to get used to. "We'll go home soon. I need to be here."

"I know." She smiled up at her father. Getting stuck into work suited her a lot more than going home thinking about Tiny.

The door closed behind him, and she sat back. Pressing on the fan she let what little cool air was over her. She felt like she was burning inside. Lifting the skirt of her dress up to her thighs, she tried to cool down. Nothing was happening.

Leaning back in her chair, she closed her eyes and moaned as she stroked her hand down her breast. Her nipple hardened against her own fingertips. Memory of Tiny's rough hands pinching her breast struck her hard. Lust pooled at her core. Pressing her thighs together, she bit her lip to contain her moan.

"You look good," Gavin said.

She'd been so deep in her fantasy she'd not heard the office door open. Sitting up, she saw Gavin staring down at her. Opening the desk drawer she pulled out an elastic band to tie her hair up to get it off her neck.

"What do you want, Gavin?" she asked, staring down at the books in front of her.

"We've never got a chance to talk. You walked away, and I was left waiting and wondering when you were coming home." He closed the door giving them privacy. Some of the men outside knew her past.

Looking up, Eva was thankful when she felt nothing for him.

"What do you want to know?" she asked, picking up a pencil to hold. She hated her hands being left empty, especially when she was filled with lust for a man who wasn't anywhere near.

"How have you been?" He sat opposite her.

"Fine. How have you been?"

She could be nice and complimentary all he needed.

"Good."

"Okay, so we're both good, and I take it nothing eventful has happened in our lives," she said, shrugging. "What else do you want to know?" The conversation was stilted, and to be honest, she wanted to be left alone with her own thoughts.

"I missed you."

"I'm sure there were more than enough women to make up for my absence."

"For fuck's sake, Eva, stop being fucking difficult."

Dropping the pencil she stood up to glare at him. "I've not come back home for any dying need to be with you, Gavin. I'm hoping you've got a woman of your own."

"No, I haven't. I've been waiting for you to come back."

"Then you were waiting wrong. I'm not your woman, Gavin, and I never was."

He stood and rounded the desk to stand beside her. With her hair up, she left her neck exposed. Gavin took full advantage, dropping his lips to her neck.

Nothing turned within her. Tingles started at where he kissed, but nothing like desire pulled within her. Anyone could touch her neck, and she'd be affected.

"We used to be so good together." His hand went to her stomach.

Spinning in his arms, she pressed a hand to his chest. "We used to be good together. I belong to someone else, Gavin. I'm not yours."

He released her, taking a step back. "I'm sorry."

"What for?" she asked.

"For screwing around on you. It's my one biggest regret with you." He reached out to push a strand of hair that she'd missed off her face. "If I could take it back I would."

Rolling her eyes she stepped away. "She wasn't the only one, was she?"

He looked down giving her all the answer she needed.

"See, we were not supposed to be together." Closing the books, she placed everything away where her father showed her.

"We can still be friends," he said.

"I know. You've got to stop trying to be something more. We're over, Gavin." She went to the door.

"This new man, is this a Skull?" Gavin asked.

Glancing over her shoulder she saw the anger in his eyes. "Yes, it is."

"Who?"

"You know The Skulls?" she asked.

"Not personally. I know Ned does business through them."

Good, she would hate for Gavin to know Tiny.

"Yes, he's a Skull." Stepping out of the door, she turned back to smile at him. "It's Tiny."

Closing the door, she went to her father. "Where are we staying tonight?" she asked.

Ned handed her a key card. "You've got a room at Alex Allen's casino."

Taking the key card from him, she headed out into the night. The sun had set during her time in the gym. Keeping her head down, she walked toward the casino in no hurry to be trapped in another room that made her feel like a stranger.

****

The drug run went by without a hitch, and it had been a week since Eva had left him. He'd been in contact with her by text, but it wasn't the same as getting to see her every day. Sitting down in a chair at the table he watched Hardy and Rose dance together. Rose was naked, again, with Hardy teasing and tormenting her for all the men to see.

Everyone was high from the ride on the bikes. He'd left his to get some repairs in the shop. Tiny only ever trusted his men to work on his bike.

"How are you doing, boss?" Zero asked, taking a seat beside him. The bruises on Zero's face were fading fast. Killer sat at the bar, drinking and keeping everyone away from him. Even Whizz and Time hadn't gotten close to the other man.

"I'm doing good. It's always good after a ride to get shit into order." Nothing had happened transporting the drugs. The rush was still there for a safe journey, but the excitement of returning home wasn't there.

"It's not the same without Eva. She always had

some food waiting, and we had a little party at your house," Zero said.

"I know. You're going to have to get used to these parties. Eva is not coming back."

Sandy and Stink were sat on the couch at the opposite end of the room. Any remains of the pink decorations from the baby shower were gone. Tate hadn't come around since Eva's departure. He went to visit her at Murphy's house. The other brother didn't like how his woman was acting at Eva's disappearance.

"Everything is changing."

"Are you still good for our run in two weeks?"

"Yeah, are you sure we should be doing this run?" Zero asked.

"What makes you questions it?" Tiny sipped at his beer and glanced at his man.

"I don't know. Something just feels fucking off about it. Ignore me, boss. I need some pussy." Zero left him alone.

Zero's obsession with Sophia had left the man a shell of his former self. He remembered a time when Zero would do nothing but tease and chase pussy.

He left the room to go to his office. Locking the door, he settled behind his desk, running his fingers over the spot where Eva had sat on the edge. He could taste her on his lips.

Grabbing his phone, he dialed her number.

"Hello," she said. He heard her yawn over the line.

"Hello, baby."

Hearing her voice made him hotter than hell.

"Tiny? Is that you?"

"Who else would be phoning you?"

She was moving around. The sound of a light switch going on let him know she was in bed.

"Have you come off of one of your runs?" she asked.

"Yeah."

"Are your boys missing my cooking?" She chuckled at his grunt.

"You know us all so well. We miss you, Eva."

"I miss you, too."

"Then come home."

She was silent at his request. Damn, stubborn woman. Why wouldn't she give in and give him what he wanted?

"What are you wearing?" he asked, more curious about her naked state.

"A black negligee."

"Panties?"

"Tiny—"

"Panties?" he asked again. Tiny wasn't going to give in to her.

"I'm not wearing any."

He paused, staring ahead of him at the blank door. Running a hand down the front of his pants, he closed his eyes imagining her in the negligee he'd seen in her drawers when she lived with him, without any underwear on.

"Tiny, are you still there?" she asked.

"Yeah, baby, I'm still here."

"What are you doing?" Her voice sounded breathless to him.

"I'm touching my dick, staring at my desk where I tasted your sweet pussy."

Her moan echoed down the line. "You're not playing fair."

"I never play fair. Not when it's what I want, and Eva, I want you."

The noise she made sounded muffled almost as if

she'd buried her head into the pillow.

"Touch yourself," he said, ordering her what to do.

"What? Why?"

Smiling, he flicked the button open on his jeans and lowered them down to his knees. Peeling away his boxer briefs he gripped the erect flesh of his shaft.

"Do what I say." He stroked the length, wishing she was near so he could give her what he wanted to give her.

She whimpered, and he knew her hand was between her sweet thighs.

"Are you wet?"

"We're seriously going to do this? Have phone sex?" she asked.

"I'd rather sink into your tight pussy, but this is all I can have from you."

"What about the sweet-butts?"

"They're over, baby. No more sweet-butts and no more women. I only want you." Tiny knew what he spoke was the truth. There was no other woman he wanted other than the one he was speaking to. "Touch yourself. Press those fingers through your slit."

He waited for her to comply. Hearing her move across the phone line was frustrating and arousing at the same time.

"I'm touching myself," she said, moaning.

"Are you wet?"

"Yes, I want you, Tiny."

Licking his lips, he fisted his shaft imagining her hands wrapped around him. In his mind he saw Eva knelt before him, ready to take his cock.

"I'm hard for you, Eva."

"I'd love to feel you in my mouth, Tiny."

He groaned, wishing her plump lips were

wrapped around his shaft. "Finger your clit, stroke yourself."

"I want you." She cried out, and he pumped at his shaft. He felt her yearning deep in his soul. The intensity of his feelings made him feel like he was going to drown on his need for her alone.

"Put two fingers inside you and stretch them out."

Her cries turned to guttural moans. Pre-cum leaked out of the tip of his cock, coating his shaft.

"I bet you're tight. I know you are. You're tight enough for my cock and only my cock."

"Yes, I'm all yours. There's no one else."

He growled, feeling the first bite of his orgasm. His balls tightened, and he kept stroking. She screamed over the line. The sound of her release set him over the edge with his own orgasm.

Coming down from the high, he was panting for breath.

"Wow, there is a first for anything," Eva said.

Tiny chuckled. "I'd rather fuck you in the flesh, baby. This was the next best thing."

"Give me a second. Don't go." Eva left the phone, and he heard her walking around and the sound as she jarred her foot. "Fuck that hurt."

Minutes passed, and she was finally over the line. "Sorry, I was washing my hands and taking a quick bathroom break."

Smiling, he reached for some tissue from the edge of his desk to clean up the mess he'd created.

"How is Vegas?" he asked, not wanting the conversation to end. The times he'd fucked women, even Patricia, he'd not been interested in talking afterward. With Eva, he never wanted the moment to end.

"Vegas is fast moving, hot as hell, and a pain in the ass. The fighters my father has with him are right rough necks. I think you and your boys could take them though." She laughed over the line. "I'd probably be given the boot if they heard me saying that."

"And you're staying with Ned?" Tiny asked.

"For now. I don't know what else to do. Everything seemed so clear when I was with you in Fort Wills. Getting out of town was the ideal solution to our problem." Eva stopped, and he imagined her running fingers through her hair.

"What do you think now?" He threw the used towels in the trash. Resting his head against his shoulder, he pulled up his jeans, fixing them back in place.

"We were toxic to each other, Tiny. Nothing has changed."

"I promise you, Eva, there are no more women. I swear down on my life and the life of my club." He leaned on the desk, resting his hand under his chin.

"We've hurt each other—"

"This was because I was a fucking dick who didn't know how to deal with my feelings."

"I can't believe you've just admitted you were a dick. Does Tate have you at gun point?"

"No, Eva. I've finally come to my senses." He stopped, needing to collect himself before he started shouting once again.

He heard her heavy sigh over the line. "You're spoiling it again."

"I'm not. For fuck's sake, I'm trying to make this work between us. You left before I got chance to get my head screwed on straight."

She growled over the line. "So this is all my fucking fault? What about you? Don't you remember all those other women you fucked? Or the way you treated me? I was not your woman, but I wasn't allowed a life of my own."

Tiny refused to drag in the fact they were not actually together, especially when he'd put the word out for no one to touch her because she was his.

"Fuck, you're making me angry. See, this is why we'd never work. You say something that just pisses me the fuck off."

"Baby, I love it when you're angry." Their life together would be passionate, fiery, and would never be a dull moment.

"You're an asshole."

"I love you." He'd never told her how he felt.

Tiny expected the silence over the line. He gave her time to process what he just said.

"Are you still alive?" he asked.

"You love me?"

"Yes."

"Is this some kind of fucking trick?"

"No, no trick. I love you, Evangeline Walker. I'll take the ass kicking your father is going to give me. I want you by my side … as my wife."

She squeaked, and he heard something crash to the floor.

"Eva? Eva, are you all right?"

"Shit, I just fell off the bed."

He laughed. No wonder this woman and Tate got on so well. They were like two peas in the pod.

"Is this for real?" she asked.

"Pinch yourself, and you tell me."

"Ouch, crap this is all real."

"Well, will you?" He tensed, waiting.

"I really don't know, Tiny."

She hadn't said she loved him back.

Nodding his head, Tiny thumped his forehead, remembering she couldn't see him. "Okay, I'm not going to beg for an answer right now. I want you to take some time to think about everything. Promise me, Eva. Promise me when you have an answer, I want you to think about it clearly."

"You're the first man to ask me to marry you, Tiny. I'm not going to jump in."

"I love you. Our life would be here. I'd want you to wear my ring and my cut. This will not be a quiet affair, baby. We'll have it all, the wedding, the honeymoon, and I'll have your name inked on my skin."

"Oh, Tiny." From the sounds she was making, he knew she was sobbing.

"Think about it. I'll be waiting, and you know how to reach me." He hung up the phone, staring straight ahead as he thought about what he'd done.

Eva was the first woman since Patricia that he admitted to being in love with, and she hadn't said anything to give him hope. From the first moment he saw Patricia he'd been in love with her. She had been everything he needed at the time, sweet, innocent, pure. For most of his early years he'd only dealt with anger, rage, and death. Being part of The Darkness had guaranteed that. When he'd gone to Alex for help in taking over Fort Wills, he'd fallen for her and never looked back. But with Eva the feelings were even more intense, and he'd denied them for so long. He knew deep down that she had to love him.

It's Eva. She loves me.

Chapter Eight

Two weeks later

Eva stared at the phone on the desk in her father's office. She'd been talking with Tate off and on along with Tiny. Nothing else was mentioned of his proposal. She still couldn't believe he'd proposed.

Looking down at the envelope, Eva didn't know why she was holding back. She loved the man, and he'd sent her a ring. A fucking engagement ring glinted at her from the envelope she'd opened. Inside lay a letter on plain white paper.

They talked on the phone every night, the phone sex occurring every night, and her body was alive with what he could ask her to do. She pulled the sheet of paper out of the envelope and opened it up. Tiny had written the letter himself.

Eva,

I love you with my whole heart. Words have never been great with me nor to speak them. I've been married before, and I had to bury her. I'm not looking for a replacement wife. I want you, no one else. If you turn into a bitch, then I'll trade you in ☺ (joke). I know you still haven't answered me, and this is not me trying to force you to answer.

You're the first woman I ever wanted since my wife. You're good through and through. What I've done over the last eight years of us knowing each other, is wrong. I should be fucking castrated for what I've done to you. I hope you won't tell your father to cut my dick off. I'm quite partial to it. Also, you cut my dick off and our wedded life won't be much fun, just saying.

Anyway, try the ring on. See how it feels. I want to do right by you. There is no other woman for me. The sweet-butts are over. You have all of me, Eva. My heart, body, mind, and soul are yours, no matter how jaded I am.

> *I love you, and that will never change.*
> *Tiny (Maximus)*

"What are you doing?" Gavin asked, walking into the office.

She held the letter close to her chest, staring down at the silver band with the small diamond in the center. There was nothing large or garish about it. Picking the ring up, she slid it onto her finger, ignoring Gavin. He grabbed a bottle of water from the fridge in the corner, taking a seat on the only sofa near the door. From his position he wouldn't be able to see what she was doing.

"Earth to Eva."

Glaring at him, she glanced in his direction. "What?"

"You've been staring down at the desk. I was wondering what has your attention."

In the last two weeks Gavin had been trying to woo her. She really wasn't interested. Lifting her hand up, she showed him the ring, which happened to fit perfectly on her finger. "Tiny has asked me to marry him."

The mouthful of what he'd been sipping spat out of his mouth. She was far enough away so she wasn't covered.

"Holy shit," Ned said, walking into the office. "Has Gavin proposed?"

"No, Tiny has."

She dropped her hand to the desk, staring at the note then at the ring. Circling the ring on her finger, she started to take it off and then realized she didn't want to. Licking her lips, she read the note again. She would keep it on to see how it felt.

You're torturing him without an answer.

Time, he'd offered her time, and it was time she needed to get her thoughts together. Marriage was a big step.

"Eva, you better not make a rash decision," Ned said.

"I'm not going to."

"Gavin, get the fuck out of my office."

"Gladly." The other man stormed out as Ned closed the door.

She wasn't scared or startled by the way he was reacting. "What's this about, Dad?" she asked.

"Tiny asked you to marry him in a fucking letter?" Ned asked. He made to grab the letter from her. She stopped him. The letter Tiny sent to her was personal. There was no way she would be letting her father see the words.

"No, he asked me to marry him several nights ago. What's your problem with him?"

"He's not right for you."

"You were trying to convince me to stay with him back in Fort Wills. What changed?" she asked, curious to know.

"I finally got you back. You stay with Tiny, and then I know for damn sure I won't get to see you. Gavin is a lot better. You can stay here, and I can keep an eye on you, protect you."

"And Gavin the cheating fuck is better for me because you get to keep me around?" She stood up, glaring at him.

"He's better for you than that fucking biker," Ned said, yelling.

"Why? Because Gavin knows the business whereas my *fucking biker* doesn't give a fuck about your business or how you live your life?" She stared at her father seeing the answer glaring at her in the face. "That's it, isn't it? You want me to marry *Gavin* because you want someone to take over what you started."

"Honey, I love you, but this," he gestured all around him, "is my life. I put everything I have in this club, and I made sure you'd be protected for the rest of your life."

She shook her head. "No, this is not going to be about you or this fucking club."

Staring down at her hand Eva knew she was going to marry Tiny. The only problem she had was when she was going to tell him.

"I've never asked you for much, Dad. I never asked about my mother, and I was always with you in the beginning—"

"You left, Eva. I've got no son, and you're not a fighter. The men respect you, but you're not a fighter. These men need a fighter."

Tears filled her eyes. "No, I'm not going to be marrying Gavin. I love Tiny."

"Tiny's on a drug run, honey. He's a criminal, and when he gets caught he'll be punished for it. Will you be waiting around for him to come home from prison?"

She laughed. "Dad, you run an underground fighting ring with known runs with The Skulls. You can go to prison at any time. Gavin can go as well. Either way, I sit around waiting for one man or the other."

Eva rounded the desk and walked toward her father. "I love you, Dad. This decision is not yours to make." She wrapped her arms around his neck and hugged him close. "I'm off for the day."

Moving away, she passed all the men fighting. No one stopped her as she made her way toward the door. Several women were watching the men fight. She knew they were fighter groupies for the men. They followed each fight in the hope of landing one of them. Eva had dealt with her fair share of followers. Heading out into the hot warm air she didn't think of where she was going.

There was no destination in mind, and she stopped in a diner, going to the back for some privacy. She ordered a milkshake and pulled out the letter Tiny had left her.

Next she grabbed her cell phone and dialed his number.

"I was wondering when you were going to call," Tiny said, answering on the third ring.

"You never told me to expect something in the mail."

"It wouldn't have been a surprise if I had." There was a pause. "Do you like it?"

"Yes, I do."

"Do you have it on?" he asked.

"Yeah, I've got the ring on." She was staring at the small diamond.

"I picked it out. None of my boys know, and this is between you and me." Tiny was out in the open. She heard the purr of the bikes.

"What are you up to?" she asked, thinking about the compound with all The Skulls ready to go on a run.

"We've got a drop off to do. I don't want to hear your answer until I get back. It'll give me something to think about on the open road."

"I can tell you now," she said.

"Nah, I'm not in the mood to spoil the surprise. Either way, Eva, baby, you have my heart."

Smiling, she accepted the drink from the waitress.

"You're being an ass."

"Why? Do you really want to tell me?" he asked.

"Yes, I do." She glanced around the diner wishing with all of her might that she was in Fort Wills, looking at him. "I wish I was with you."

"That's another thing, baby, we do this, and you're staying with me. Fort Wills will be your home."

"Good. I look forward to it."

"Yo, Tiny, we've got to go."

"Was that Stink?" she asked.

"Yeah. He's taking care of Sandy at the minute. She's staying at the compound until we come back," Tiny said.

"Smart move. I'm sure I've seen Stink looking at her with something more than sex on the brain." She sipped at her drink.

"I'm more than just a pretty face."

"I know you are," she said, remembering the feel of him between her thighs.

He growled. "You've got me thinking about fucking you."

"Good. You'll know how I feel then." She smiled, feeling an answering heat of her own. The phone sex they'd shared was fun, but it wasn't going to do the job.

"I've got to go. This run needs to be done today. I love hearing your voice," he said.

"Okay, I'll let you go, but you ride safe, you hear." She gave the warning not wanting anything to happen to him.

"Baby, knowing you're waiting for me is all I need to hear."

He hung up, and she stared down at her cell phone, wishing there was something more she could do. She hated not knowing what was happening or if there was anything more she could do.

Tiny wouldn't let anything happen to him. His men, the club were all important to him.

****

"Something doesn't feel right about this," Murphy said, putting his helmet on. Tate and the women were not invited to see them off this time. Tiny had requested no women as this was one of their biggest shipments, and he didn't want anything to go wrong. Usually only a handful of the boys carried the load to their destination whereas today all of them were carrying.

It was a risky shipment, but he'd never backed down from an order. This was his life, and it kept his town clean.

"Everything will be fine. We've got no choice. After this one we're on hold for a few months," Tiny said.

"None of this makes any sense," Lash said. "Every run is spaced out, yet this one is on a specific route. Tiny, we never got the route we're ordered to."

Tiny slashed his arm down. "Look!" His voice carried, and all the bikers stopped. "This is what we've been ordered to do. We've got no choice but to see it through otherwise we're up shit creek. Alex deals with the order, and this is what he's said. They want this specific route or no deal."

When Tiny was told there was a route requested by the dealers he'd wanted to turn it away. Alex didn't feel there was a problem as the supply was coming from Ned Walker. Tiny wasn't about to tell Eva who he was running for. Alex was happy with Ned, and the supplier didn't seem to have any priors and it certainly didn't sound like a trap.

Still, he understood his men's anxiety for this run.

Every other run they made their own path and got the job done. "Sandy's at home, and if anything happens we can return to plan B and our failsafe. Never forget to be prepared, boys. I'm always prepared for on the road." He kept prospects and some of the women at the compound during runs for a reason. They were his failsafe if something was to go wrong.

"Let's ride." He straddled his bike, turning the key in the ignition and kicked off. Tiny was in front of all of his boys as they made their way out of Fort Wills. The route was ingrained in his mind, and he wasn't going to be forgetting about it anytime soon. He'd never taken the route before as he liked to map his own destination. Two hours passed, and they made their first stop to get some food, fill the bikes and recoup.

Unlike so many other runs this one was silent. No one was saying a word as they went about their business.

Tiny didn't like the silence. He was uscd to his men messing around and fussing around. Murphy stared at his cell while Nash and Lash were muttering to each other. They had vulnerable women at home.

Shouldn't have let them come.

All three men had wanted to go. It would be one of their last rides in the coming months as they all wanted to stay at home. Lash, Murphy, and Nash wanted this final run, and then they were out until after their babies were born.

He ignored the warning, got back on his bike and started back on the road. The journey was another three hours in when the road darkened. An incline was to his right with trees and what looked like a forest to his left. There were no track marks on the road, and Tiny felt the hairs on the back of his neck stand on end. He slowed the bike down, and in his mirror he saw the boys do the same.

Something was off. His senses were on high alert. Tiny didn't have the first clue what was going on or why he was feeling concerned. His piece was down by his leg out of reach as he concentrated on the road.

The first bullet ricochets off his bike. He jerked at the impact. Out of his mirror he saw the other bikes coming from the distance. Tiny couldn't focus, and then chaos ensued. Out of the corner of his eye he saw Lash and Nash crash off their bikes seconds before they blew up.

Seeing those boys hit the tarmac made Tiny sick to his stomach. He slipped and skidded off his bike as another wave of bullets hit. His leg hit the tarmac scraping along. He was pulled off and landed on the hard ground next to the trees. His leg, back, and arm were on fire, but he didn't give himself chance to assess the damage. The pain was excruciating. Glancing over the grass verge, he saw Lash stand and take a bullet to the thigh. The men were still coming on their bikes. The guns glinted in the sunlight. The attack on The Skulls was intentional. Tiny couldn't move.

"Failsafe," he said, hoping his men could hear him. One by one he watched his men fall all around him. Killer was charged off his bike at the back. He didn't see what happened as Killer stood and started to fight. They were all outnumbered, and there was nothing any of them could do.

Zero was on the ground, grunting. Butch was trying his best to hold on, and Murphy's bike was down and burning with no signs of the other man. It was a bloodbath, and Tiny couldn't wait to see what happened. Getting up from his position he headed into the trees. His cell phone was by his leg, and he pulled it out.

He quickly dialed Alex's number."

"Hello, I thought you weren't—"

"It's a trap."

"The cops are there?" Alex asked.

"No, another fucking club." He glanced behind him in time to see the symbol he hoped to never see again. Tiny recognized the symbol for The Darkness, and he knew in that instant Snitch was alive.

"This couldn't be. I know Ned, and he wouldn't fucking betray me," Alex said.

"He may not know. Where are you?" Tiny asked.

"I'm in Vegas."

Tiny nodded as he heard a scream that sounded a lot like Stink. "My men are dying out there. I don't know who survived, but I'm implementing the failsafe. You've got to make sure Tate is fine."

"She's pregnant, Tiny. I can't give her that news. She might lose the baby."

Cursing, Tiny knew he wouldn't be able to tell his daughter or any of the women. "Then you make sure they've got an eye on them. I'll call you when I can. I'm destroying this phone."

"What? Why?" Alex asked.

"It's Snitch, and he'll know how to track me even when I don't want him to." Without waiting, he slammed the cell phone against the trunk of the tree. He needed to get moving otherwise they were all going to be dead. Taking a step away, he gasped as the pain was unbearable.

Keep moving.

His leg was bleeding from being scraped along the tarmac. The jeans and protective leathers he'd worn had saved him from a lot of the damage, but even he knew they weren't fucking invincible.

Checking behind him, Tiny hated leaving his men, but it was something they all agreed on. From the beginning nothing had changed. They'd all agreed if they were attacked they got out. The same discussion never changed even when new men had joined. Blaine, Killer,

Whizz, Time, and Steven had all agreed with the terms.

If at any time they were hit by the cops or by another biker group and were outnumbered they had to disband and get out of harm's way. No one stayed behind. Their life depended on them leaving and regrouping at a later date. Until today Tiny had never had to leave his men behind. He felt like a coward, and yet there was nothing for him to do. If he tried to take on the men, he'd be dead before he made the first kill. Tiny sent a prayer to whatever God listened to him to keep his men safe. Pulling his gun from his leg he started walking.

During the walk he didn't give a fuck about the pain. He didn't know how long he was walking until he stumbled upon a small town.

People gave him a wide berth, which he didn't mind. When he got to the phone he pushed some money into the slot and typed in Devil's number. He'd always been good at remembering numbers.

"Who the fuck is this?" Devil asked, clearly angry.

"Tiny, I need your help." He wouldn't be talking to the leader of Chaos Bleeds if it wasn't necessary.

"What do you need now? Your man, Whizz, he pulled through. I found her sister, and I'm having the fucking party of a lifetime—"

Tiny wished he had all the time in the world to listen to his friend, but he didn't. "Snitch is back."

Silence fell from his interruption.

"Are you fucking shitting me?" Devil asked.

"Wish I was, but on a drug run all my crew and I were just attacked. I don't know who survived, but it was a fucking ambush." Tiny detailed everything even down to the planned route.

"Sounds to me Alex has it in for you," Devil said.

"Nah, this was fucking planned. Snitch is back,

and he's after revenge. He wants me out of the fucking picture, and the only way to do that is to get rid of me and my crew." Tiny tore some of his shirt to wrap around his bleeding knuckles.

"Shit, with Snitch back it affects all of us. I'll gather some guys together and come help you out."

"Not right away. Wait for my phone call. This needs to be handled properly." Tiny spat on the ground and saw one of his teeth mixed in. Fuck, he was getting too fucking old for this shit.

"What do you think Snitch will do?" Devil asked.

"He wants Fort Wills. I'm sure now he was the one responsible for trying to put Nash and Sophia in the ground. It's now our job to make sure he goes to fucking ground."

"Whatever you need, it's yours."

"Good. Stand by for my call."

"With pleasure," Devil said, hanging up. He needed to get to Vegas, and only then could he find out who of his men were alive, if any at all.

****

One day later

Killer held onto his side as he kept to the shadows. His side hurt like hell, and his cell remained eerily silent. Fort Wills didn't look too terrifying as he walked past closed shops and empty streets. It was night time, and no one was wandering around. Whatever was going on hadn't reached the town yet.

Since the attack where he'd taken three men on he'd been hitching rides off passing people. Some people stopped just to be nosey. He paid them money for the ride back to Fort Wills. No one would enter the dangerous biker town, and he had to walk the rest of the way otherwise he'd have gotten home far sooner.

Leaning against a dumpster he took several

breaths to gain composure. He'd not slept in over twenty-four hours, and he was feeling it.

Rounding a corner he went straight for the intercom on Kelsey's building.

"Hello?" Her sweet voice came over the line.

"Kels, I need you to buzz me in."

He heard her sigh, but the sound of the buzzer filled him with relief. She was waiting by her door as he walked down to her. Killer still held onto his side. As he walked into the light he saw the change within her. He knew he didn't look all that appealing.

"Killer? What happened?" Kelsey asked, going to him.

Stumbling into her apartment, he shut and locked the door. Pulling the gun from his pants, he placed it on the counter near the door.

"You should see the other guy," he said, joking.

When he was satisfied no one had followed him, he started to remove his jacket. His side was patched up the best he could, but he wasn't doing good.

"You're bleeding. Crap, what is going on?" Kelsey asked, helping him into a seat. He found her caring endearing.

Pulling his shirt over his head, he sat down as she bustled around the kitchen. "I came to you. I thought you would be more qualified to stitch me up." Partly the truth. After what he'd just been through he didn't want any other woman's hands on him other than Kelsey's.

"I'm a dental nurse, Killer."

"Don't care. You'll do a better job than I ever will. I'll probably give myself an infection and die."

She walked over carrying her first aid lit. Kelsey grabbed his face. "Don't ever say anything like that." Releasing him she set about working on his side. "What caused this?"

"Dodged a bullet only the fucker grazed me."

"Do I need to call Tate and the others?" she asked.

He reached for her, holding her hand. "No, you don't call anyone. I need you to keep my presence a secret until I know more."

"You're scaring me. What the hell is going on?"

Letting out a sigh, Killer stared at her exposed shoulder. She was in her nightwear. He loved the look of her pale flesh. Reaching out he pressed a hand to her shoulder seeing the muck and grime all over him. Before he could touch her, he pulled his hand away.

"We were attacked. It was a run, a standard drop off. We've done them loads of times, but this was different. The route was planned, and all of us had the product strapped to the bikes." He winced as she started to clean his wound. "Fuck, it stings."

"I'm sorry. I'm being as careful as I can."

"I don't know who they fucking were. I've never seen them before in my life. They were another fucking crew."

"Where are the others?" Kelsey asked, putting the soiled bandages into a pot of water.

"We spread out. We've got a deal that if we're ambushed or outnumbered we move … scatter."

"Do you know who survived? You've got a bullet wound. There have to have been casualties, Killer." She applied some antiseptic to the area. He held onto the edge of the counter to stop himself from screaming at the excruciating pain.

"I don't know. I saw Tiny come off his bike. He's going to be fucking messed up even though he was wearing the proper shit. I saw him head off to the tree line. I saw Lash and Nash go down. I couldn't stop it. The brothers went down together. I didn't see anyone else. They could all be out on that road and dead. I got away and was able to escape." He still couldn't believe how lucky he was. After he'd injured or dazed the men attacking him, he'd run like hell.

"Angel and Sophia are expecting."

"I know. I was there, Kels. I couldn't do anything. We were surrounded. Blaine is gone as well, and he's got the start of a family and he's been dealing with his shit." He cursed and slammed his fist against the counter. Killer wanted to hurt everyone who'd taken his club away from him.

"What about Murphy? Tate's my best friend."

Killer swallowed. "Last I saw his bike exploded. I don't know if he was on it or not."

Kelsey pressed a hand to her lips.

"Zero was hit as well. I don't know, Kels. Fuck, I didn't see anyone who made it out."

"What do we do?" she asked.

"I've got to wait for a signal of what we do next. If Tiny's alive, he'll be in touch."

She sobbed. "Tate could have lost the father of her child and her own father." Tugging her in close, Killer wrapped his arms around her shoulders, trying his best to console her.

"I'll do what I need to do to keep you safe." Kissing her head, he promised himself every single bastard who hurt his club would die.

Chapter Nine

The following day Killer was staring out of the apartment window when he saw Kelsey running toward the building. Grabbing his gun from beside him, he tucked it away and met her downstairs. She was out of breath, and tears were falling from her eyes.

"What is it?" he asked, holding her close.

"The compound … it's on fire. The fire and rescue service are trying to put it out, but it's useless."

This was it. Only a Skull could organize the burning of The Skull compound. He was escorting her back into the building when Tate pulled up with Sophia and Angel. All three women looked frantic.

Tate ran up to him, shoving him hard.

"What the fuck is going on? I can't get hold of Murphy anywhere, and you were supposed to be on the run with him." He stared at all four women. Shit, he really had to get them all to calm down.

"Come inside. I'll explain everything."

Kelsey started to make drinks as Killer told the expectant women everything he knew. Angel broke down.

"No, I can't do this without Lash. He's supposed to be here."

Tate was frozen to the spot. Kelsey's hands were shaking as she brought over the drinks.

"His bike blew up?" Tate asked.

"Yes. He could still be alive, Tate. You need to keep your shit together right now. Tiny had a plan for everything—"

"He didn't have a fucking plan for being attacked by fucking bikers. My father and husband are missing, Killer. They're *missing*."

"You can yell at me all you want to, Tate, but I

can't change anything that has happened."

Killer took a sip of his drink.

"Someone was ordered to burn the compound to the ground?" Angel asked.

"Yes. We've got rules in place. All of us have a job to do."

Tate's phone went. Killer paused as she answered. He heard her give directions to Kelsey's house.

"It's Sandy. She's on her way."

Tears tracked down Tate's cheeks. He hoped to God that Murphy survived.

"He's got to be alive. I know my man, and he wouldn't put himself in danger," Angel said.

"He's got Nash," Sophia said. "They're brothers. They'll get through it together."

He listened to the woman console themselves as the intercom buzzed. Kelsey let Sandy up to her apartment. Moments of silence passed as they all waited for the other woman to get to them.

Her knock sounded, and Kelsey let her inside. Killer was surprised to see how dirty she was, and she held a black bag.

"What happened to you?" Kels asked.

Sandy closed the door, much like he had the night before. "I, erm, I've been given orders to come here and give you this."

Killer stared at the bag. "What happened?"

"Stink called me and gave me instructions that have come from Alex. I was asked to empty out the safes and torch the place after getting everyone out of the compound." Sandy was shaking as she handed over the bag. "He told me to take a couple of grand and go and to give the rest to you."

Tate took the bag and looked inside. "What is all

this?"

"It's a failsafe for us. Stink is alive. He doesn't know who else is. Alex got in contact with him and then told him to destroy his phone."

Killer looked down at his phone and destroyed it quickly. Fuck, it was one of the first things he was supposed to do. No one glanced his way as Sandy held their attention.

"Where are you going?" Kelsey asked.

"I'm heading out. Stink told me to get out of Fort Wills. I'm taking his advice and getting out. I've been given a number to call, and I'll keep in contact with him."

The compound was gone. The club had dispersed, and Killer knew he could either stick to Fort Wills or run. He'd never been a coward, and he wasn't running.

"What else did Stink say?" Tate asked.

"Nothing. No one knows anything."

He watched Tate curse and start dialing a number.

"Do you want a shower? Something to eat, to sit down?" Kelsey asked.

"No, I'm going to head out. I need to get on the road. Stink was pretty adamant about it. Fort Wills is going to get dangerous, and I'm not sticking around. I've already had enough excitement to last me a lifetime." Sandy smiled, but it didn't reach her eyes.

Killer saw it was tearing her up inside. She was scared.

"I'm going to go now," she said.

Kelsey saw her to the door, and Killer turned his attention back to Tate.

"Alex is not fucking answering me." Tate growled.

"What about Eva?" Kelsey asked. "She's close to all of them, and she's in Vegas."

"Good idea. I'll talk to her."

Killer stared out of the window wondering what the hell was going on.

****

Eva listened to the number ring off once again. Tiny wasn't answering the phone, and she wasn't getting any answer from the compound. Ned and Gavin had left her in the office. For the last couple of days they'd been avoiding her. Whenever she tried to talk to them they found something else to do. The diamond ring on her finger glinted at her.

Ringing Tiny's number she growled as it once again disconnected. "For fuck's sake, Tiny, answer your fucking phone."

She slammed her cell phone down on the desk, running fingers through her hair. Eva wanted to talk to the man who proposed. The run had been yesterday, and he hadn't been in touch.

Her cell phone went off, and she answered it without looking at the screen.

"Tiny, where the fuck have you been? I've been worried sick," Eva said.

Silence was on the other end. "It's not Tiny. It's me, Tate."

The despair in the other woman's voice had Eva on alert. "Tate, what's wrong?"

"I, erm, have you heard from my dad?"

"I've not spoken to him since yesterday morning when he about to go on his latest run."

"Something bad has happened," Tate said.

Eva tensed. "What?"

The next ten minutes were the longest of her life. Her heart was breaking as Tate described every single word of what went down. Tiny could be dead. The man she loved with her heart and soul could be lying in a ditch somewhere dead.

"What are you talking about?" Eva asked, dread overcoming her and making it impossible for her to speak straight. She couldn't breathe.

She stood from behind her desk as Tate's words sank in.

"They were attacked on the road. No one knows who is alive or dead. Sandy has destroyed the compound at Stink's orders. He and Killer are the only ones we know who are alive." Tate sobbed over the line. "It was only supposed to be a quick drop, Eva. I've not heard from Murphy or my father, and I'm freaking out. Killer said it was an entire fucking club, an ambush."

Her words faded all together. *An ambush? What the fuck?* Tiny was careful. He would never lead his men into a trap.

Staring out of the office window she saw her father training with Lance. Gavin hadn't even stopped by to harass her.

Ned hadn't wanted her to be alone, and he'd brought her to the gym to work even though today was her day off. Gavin was sparring with another of the men. They had both been giving her space yet keeping her in their line of sight. What did they know? Something was wrong, and she was going to find out. She knew they had information about Tiny.

"I'll be in touch, Tate."

"Please, Eva, I think they're dead."

"No, you're not to think that," Eva said. "Your father is an intelligent man. He will not let anything happen to himself or his men, I promise you that. Everything Tiny does is to protect what he holds dear."

Hanging up the phone she stormed out to her father.

"Dad, I need a word," she said, rounding the

fighting ring where her father was stood.

"Not now, honey. Give me an hour."

Holding onto the rope she climbed onto the mat and stood in front of her father. "No, we're going to talk now."

Ned dropped his arms to look at her. "What do you want to know?"

"The Skulls were organized on a drop, your drop, the other day. No one has heard from them, why?" she asked. Her anger was building. His men closed all the doors and pushed anyone who was not close to Ned out of the door.

"Eva, we do not talk shop—"

"Killer survived," she said, interrupting him. "They were attacked. How the hell did you not know, and why is it one of your drops?"

"Be careful how you speak to me."

"Tiny is missing." Tears she'd been holding back released from her. "Tiny, Murphy, Nash, Lash, Zero, and all of his other men are missing. No one knows if they're alive. You will tell me what is going, on or so help me, I will walk out of that door and I will never have anything to do with you again." She loved her father dearly, but she would turn her back on him.

Ned stared at her clearly contemplating what to tell her.

"They were on a run like every other one when they were attacked. We don't know why or by who. Alex is back in Vegas. He's rallying his men to find out everything. Tiny was able to phone him before everything died down." He stepped forward, holding onto her arms. "You can't go back to Fort Wills."

"You don't know anything?" she asked, shoving him away.

"It's not my business to know anything. My

business is to make sure nothing is traced back to us!" Ned shouted.

Shaking her head, she turned away.

"Where are you going?" he asked.

"To someone who gives a fuck to see if he's alive." She stormed out of the gym with only one destination in mind.

Gavin followed her out. "You need to stay away from this," he said. "Whoever attacked The Skulls will not stop until all of them are dead."

"I love him, Gavin. He is my heart, my soul, my very fucking life, and he could be dead."

"He's an old man."

Fisting her hand, she slammed it against his nose. He grunted, collapsing to the floor. She landed a kick against his balls. "I don't give a fuck how old he is. Tiny is mine." Turning away from him, she ran up the street, hailing the nearest taxi. She gave the direction to Alex's casino. Running fingers through her hair, she became aware of how sticky she was. The heat made her feel sick to her stomach.

Her heart wouldn't stop racing. She needed to know what was going on with her man. The only person she knew who would care was Alex. Settling back against the car, she tapped her leg and tried to focus on everything that was happening.

Tiny could be dead.

No, she wouldn't think about losing the only man she'd ever loved.

Tiny is dead.

The driver pulled up outside of the casino. She paid him and headed straight inside. Alex's henchmen were waiting for her at the door. "Mr. Allen is expecting you."

She didn't argue and followed them toward the

TINY

elevator. Leaning against the back she stared at all of their reflections not really seeing anything.

The elevator ride didn't last long. She saw they were on the top floor to the penthouse suit. They entered in the key code to the penthouse, and she was escorted inside. Alex was sat on a plush sofa. He looked up from his laptop to see her stood there. Wiping the tears from her cheeks, Eva burst into sobs again.

"Tell me what is going on," she said. "Please, tell me. Is Tiny dead?"

"Eva," Alex said, walking toward her. He wrapped his arms around her shoulders and pulled her in close.

For several seconds she accepted his embrace, and then she remembered Tiny was still gone. "No," she said, tearing herself out of his arms. "I need to know what the fuck is happening, and I need to know now." She stamped her foot, trying to keep her emotions in check. "Tell me, Alex, tell me how a simple fucking drop has turned into The Skulls running for their lives."

"We'll talk about it—"

"No, we're going to do this now. You're the one responsible for the drops. You'll tell me if you sent the man that I love off to his death." If the answer was yes she was going to beat the shit out of him with the lamp she saw out of the corner of her eye.

Alex stared at her.

"So you do love me?"

Eva never thought she would hear that voice again. Spinning on her heel she saw the man she loved. Tiny, the leader of The Skulls, was stood staring at her.

"You're alive?" she asked. It was a stupid question, but she needed to ask him.

"I'm alive. I'm kicking, and, Alex, if you don't get your hands off my woman I'm going to beat the shit out of you." Tiny wore a white bathrobe that she remembered were features with every room.

She couldn't hold back. Running to him, Eva threw herself into his arms. "I love you. I love you. I love you." She chanted the words over and over not caring who was watching or what they were thinking as she held onto him.

Tiny grunted as he wrapped his arms around her. He tucked his face against her neck and inhaled. "You smell so fucking good."

"When Tate told me I thought the fucking worst," she said.

"What? Tate knows?" Tiny asked, pulling away. He held her arms. She was falling apart, and yet she was the happiest she'd ever been.

"She called me. Killer and Stink are alive. Sandy has destroyed the compound."

Tiny looked over her shoulder to glare at Alex. "I told you not to answer."

"I've not answered any of her calls."

Eva explained about Killer going to Kelsey and then the others turning up.

"Fuck, I didn't want her to know." Tiny cursed, and she held onto him.

"You've got to tell her. She's pregnant, and no one has heard from Murphy or Nash and Lash or the others." She kept hold of his hand as he walked over to Alex.

"Give me your phone, and I'll talk to her now and you can leave."

"This is my casino," Alex said.

"You've got more than enough rooms, and after what you just did to me and my men, you fucking owe me."

Alex didn't argue. Tiny settled down on the sofa

as they were left alone. She dropped her head to his lap as he phoned Tate. Running her fingers up the inside of his thigh, she saw the bandages wrapped around his leg.

Twenty minutes later, he placed the phone on the sofa beside him. His hand rested on her back then moved up to her hair.

"How long have you been here?" she asked, tracing his leg.

"I got here this morning. Everything happened yesterday afternoon. I was waiting for Alex to arrange a meet with Ned. I wasn't waiting around here without having my woman by my side. We're going to be meeting him tomorrow."

"Good answer," she said, looking up at him. "When I got that call from Tate I was so fucking scared. I thought you were dead."

"It's going to take a fucking lot to get rid of me."

She smiled even as her tears spilled over.

"Hey, no more tears." He stroked her cheek, and he winced. "I love you, babe, but you fucking stink."

He lifted her up in his arms and carried her through to the bathroom. She screamed and held onto him as he dumped her on her feet. Eva watched as he started to run her a bath. In quick movements he got her undressed.

"I don't smell."

"You smell. I'm not touching you until you wash that smell off you." He ran his hands up and down her thighs.

"What smell is that?" she asked.

"The smell of dirty fucking fighters."

Laughing, Eva didn't know how she could be happy at a time like this.

****

Tiny stayed out of the bath as he dumped Eva

inside. She gasped and laughed. He was so happy to see her. When he'd arrived that morning looking like shit he'd only wanted to go see her. Alex refused to give him the directions. The bastard had made him get settled, have a wash, and be seen by his personal doctor. His legs were a mess from coming off his bike, but the doctor had taken care of him. Everything was bandaged up, and he had a special vial of pain pills in case of emergencies.

He lifted her arm seeing the engagement band he'd sent her. "Are you going to give me your answer?" he asked.

"Yes, Tiny. I'll marry you." She knelt beside the edge of the tub wrapping her arms around him. "Why can't you join me?" she asked.

"I've hurt myself, baby. I hurt bad." He removed the robe showing her what he'd done. "I can't get it wet, and I can only take sponge baths and showers where I keep it out of the way for a couple of weeks until it has all healed."

"Oh, you get a sponge bath?"

"Only until it's healed. I feel like an old fucking man."

She reached down, gripping his shaft. "You're not an old man where it counts."

Covering her hand with his, he tightened her fist. "If you're going to start playing with me then do it right."

Eva smiled. "I've missed you."

"We've been screwing since you left."

She threw her head back, laughing. "That's phone sex. It's not the same."

He agreed. Taking her hand away from his cock, he finished washing the sweat and dirt from her. Neither of them spoke while he washed her hair and helped her out of the bath. He toweled her dry then wrapped her in a bathrobe similar to his.

Together they settled on the large bed with Eva between his thighs as he brushed her hair. The wet length coated his front. He didn't mind. Feeling her hair, Tiny felt peace come over him.

"Do you know who ambushed you?" she asked, filling the silence.

Tiny didn't tense. He'd been waiting for the question and was surprised it took her so long to ask. "Yes, I know them, or at least I know the man leading them."

"You don't have to tell me what you don't know," she said.

"No, I'm going to tell you. There's never going to be any secrets between us." He moved the robe off her legs and touched her skin to skin. "I need you to promise me not to hold my past against me."

"I wouldn't do that."

He took a deep breath and looked down into her face. "Fort Wills was once an awful place to live. No one gave a fuck about the town. There was a select group known as The Darkness who ruled the town." He stopped to lick his lips. "I was part of the group with Devil and Mikey. We worked within the group fucking people up and doing whatever we wanted. I thought it was great. I could beat the shit out of anyone I wanted, and no one stopped me. I felt invincible. I didn't care about women or anything."

Tiny gripped her thighs needing her strength to hold onto. She covered his hands, providing her support. He'd never once told Patricia about his past.

"One night I was drinking, and it no longer felt right. I wasn't happy, and I was just going with the flow. Mikey and Devil were away from the group, and they said they couldn't handle the same old shit."

"I've got you, Tiny. I'm not moving anywhere. I'm here with you."

"I stumbled onto the men raping a woman. She was young, maybe eighteen, possibly younger. The men were taking turns hurting her. It was like the biggest wakeup call. The way they were with *her* I knew she wasn't their first, but I can tell you she was the fucking last. I vowed I would never let another woman come to harm in my town."

He didn't even realize he was crying until Eva wiped the tears away. She turned in his arms, wrapping her arms around his neck and straddling his waist. He held her tight and close.

"I've got you," she said.

Tiny inhaled her sweet scent knowing she would make everything finc.

"What happened to the girl?" she asked.

Closing his eyes he focused on the sweetness of her. "She was killed that night. I don't know who she was, but I buried her in a private plot in Fort Wills."

Eva tilted his head back, looking into his eyes. "You're nothing like your past."

"I hurt you."

"You avenged every wrong that came to me. You wouldn't let anyone hurt or rape me. Nash had his ass kicked because of me," Eva said, holding his gaze. "I love you, Tiny. I love the man you are now, not the little shit you were back then."

"No one hurts you. I won't let them."

She smiled. "You're very determined about that." Eva leaned forward pressing her lips to his. He moaned, running his hands up and down her back.

"I never thought I'd see you again," she said.

Sinking his fingers into her damp hair, he stared into her eyes. "I can promise you, baby, whatever happens I will make damn sure I get to you."

She was crying again. He kissed both of her eyes, trying to calm her down.

Tilting her head back he kissed her neck. He sucked on her neck where her pulse was pounding. The tears fell down her cheeks, and this was the only way he knew how to calm her down.

Untying the knot of her robe he pushed the fabric from her body leaving her naked for his touch.

"What are you going to do about the others?" she asked.

He shook his head. "No, not tonight. We're going to be here together, and the problems can wait until tomorrow."

Pressing his lips to the tops of her breasts he stared into her eyes. "Tonight is going to be about us. No one needs us until tomorrow. Alex is waiting for all of my men to contact him. They'll be in touch soon enough."

She cupped his face, pressing a kiss to his lips. He moved his hands down to grip her ass. Eva moaned against him mouth. "I love you," she said.

"I'm never going to get tired of hearing that." He turned, dropping her to the bed. Pulling his robe from his shoulders, he tossed it to the floor.

"What about your injuries?" she asked, pressing a hand to his chest.

"I don't care. The only thing I care about is being inside your sweet body and fucking you hard." Slamming his lips down on hers, he plunged his tongue into her mouth. She whimpered, opening up for him. Their tongues stroked together. Arousal spiked through him, and his cock hardened. The pain killers he'd been given were fucking brilliant.

Kissing down to her neck, he sucked on her flesh,

wanting to mark her body with his touch. With his free hand, he caressed up her thigh to land on her pussy. The fine hairs of her pubis were neat, and he slipped a finger between her slit. Sliding through her folds he found her clit.

She jerked in his arms. Moving from her neck, he kissed down to her breasts. Sucking one tight nipple into his mouth, he tongued the bud feeling her body shake underneath his.

"Tiny," she said, moaning.

"I know, baby. I know."

Her fingers sank into his hair as he gave attention to the second nipple. He loved the taste and feel of her in his mouth.

"So fucking perfect." He muttered the words against her skin, knowing he would never grow bored of her fuller, sexier curves. Plunging two fingers into her core, he watched his digits disappear into her body.

"Fuck," she said.

"We'll get to that, baby. You're going to be screaming my name before the end of this day."

Adding a third finger into her cunt, he watched her take more of him. He wasn't going to go easy on her. They'd been apart for too long, and he wanted to feel her tight heat surround him.

Kneeling over her, he removed his fingers. She whimpered in protest.

"Don't worry. I'll take care of you." Kissing down her stomach, he took time on her little belly button before going to the top of her pubis. Her scent drew him closer. She smelled musky and sweet at the same time. His mouth watered for a taste of her. "I'm going to lick this pussy until you come over my tongue."

"Yes, please, Tiny, lick me." She stared at him. Her eyes were begging him to do what he promised.

Smiling, he opened her thighs wide. The lips of her sex separated showing him a clear view of heaven. Her clit was swollen and wet with arousal. Cream leaked out of her cunt showing how turned on she was. He didn't have a clear view of her ass, but he didn't care. His attention was on that swollen clit, begging for his attention.

Sliding a finger into her pussy he pressed his lips to her clit. The sounds she made let him know how desperate she'd been for him. The time they'd been separated had only enhanced their need for each other.

Chapter Ten

Eva fisted her hands in the sheets trying with all of her might to keep hold of what little sanity she possessed. His mouth and fingers were doing wicked things to her body. Their time over the phone didn't begin to compare to the feel of him in the flesh. "Please, Tiny."

He didn't let up or do anything more. Tiny teased her clit, penetrating her pussy with his fingers, working her body the way only he could. Biting into her lip, she tried to contain her squeals.

"I want to hear those screams, Eva. I'll fucking stop if you don't give me what I want," Tiny said, frustrating the hell out of her.

Lying back, staring at the ceiling, she was shaken to the core by the pleasure he was giving her. She had never felt anything like it.

Tiny released her clit, kissing his way back up her body. "I'm going to drive you crazy." He pressed his fingers coated with her cum to her lips. Eva sucked herself off him, staring into his eyes as she did. "Now, what are you going to do for me?" he asked.

"Let you hear me scream." She pouted. Eva couldn't resist.

Smiling, he went back down between her thighs. He pulled her to the edge of the bed, making her gasp. Tiny put her feet on his shoulders as he knelt on the carpet beside the bed.

"Tiny, what are you doing?"

"Getting a better view."

She didn't have time to comment as his fingers thrust inside her while his tongue attacked her clit. He stroked over her bud as he fucked her in turn. Holding onto the edge of the bed she worked her pussy against his face, wanting him to go deeper.

Then she felt his other hand stroking down the crack of her ass. He twisted his fingers inside her, touching her G-spot as he worked her clit at the same time. Eva came apart in a matter of seconds, screaming her pleasure as loud as she could. He nibbled her clit then sucked her in deep. Eva cried out, gripping the sheets.

Through her orgasm he pressed against the puckered entrance of her anus. She tensed as the sensation made her pause.

"I'm going to have you there, baby. Do you want me there?" he asked, muttering against her pussy.

"Yes," she said, surprising herself with the answer.

"Good, then relax for me." He used some of her cream to coat his fingers. She felt everything he did even his breath across the fine hairs of her pubis as he worked. "You're going to be so tight."

She kept her grip on the blanket underneath her as he pressed a finger inside. Eva resisted him, tensing up at the foreign feeling of him trying to get inside her. She knew and trusted him. Tiny would never do anything to hurt her.

"I want you to watch," Tiny said, pulling away. He rounded the bed and motioned for her to join him.

"I don't exactly know how I'm going to see you playing with my ass." She did as he asked either way. Her excitement grew even though she was about to have his finger or his cock at what she considered an out hole.

Tiny was stood in front of her a mirror, smirking. "Alex owns a casino, but he also knows what goes down in every room."

"What the hell is that supposed to mean?" she asked, kneeling on the bed, looking over her shoulder.

He gripped his cock, pressing the tip to her cunt.

"It means the world is full of horny bastards who want to get off." Tiny slammed inside her. His cock was buried all the way to the hilt with nowhere else for her to go. In the angle from the mirror she saw a little of his cock disappearing. Tiny stared down into her eyes then back at the mirror. "I'm one of those men." He pulled out of her body then went to the end of the bed. She watched him check in the mirror before pointing at where she needed to go.

"Even in sex you're bossy."

Crawling over the bed, she got into the position he wanted.

"Look," he said, pointing at the mirror. His cock stood out straight, pointing at her ass. She watched avidly as he moved up behind her. The curve of her ass was on display, and she couldn't tear her gaze away as he moved closer. In the next instance she felt and saw his cock at the same time moving inside her body. "Now that is the fucking sexiest thing I've seen. Watching you take my cock and seeing you watch is fucking hot." His hands moved to her hips without blocking her view. She couldn't look away as with one hard thrust, he was deep inside her.

They both moaned, and Tiny stared at her in the mirror.

"You're right, you're a horny bastard," she said.

He slapped her ass making her cry out.

"So fucking sexy. I'm going to spend the rest of my life fucking you." Tiny eased out of her body only to slam back inside. Over and over she watched his slick prick appear out of her body only to plunge back inside. "You're getting turned on by watching me fucking you, aren't you?" he asked.

"Yes." She closed her eyes basking in the sensation of his hard cock driving inside her. He slapped her ass twice before cupping the cheeks he'd spanked. Tiny paused inside her. His cock was as deep as it would go.

"I love this ass. It can take a spanking." He slapped the curve once again. "And it's all mine." As he opened her cheeks wide, Eva buried her head against the blanket in the hope of containing her excitement. She shouldn't be getting off on him touching and feeling up her ass.

"You're an ass man."

"You better believe it, baby." His fingers were coated with her cream, and she felt him start to press against her anus.

Her moans were muffled by the bedspread.

"Relax for me," he said.

She tried to relax, but with a cock inside her pussy and his fingers pressing against her ass, Eva felt nothing but tense.

His free hand caressed her back, going up her spine then down again. Tiny took his time, stroking her body until she slowly started to relax against his touch. She wanted every delicious and wicked part of him.

"Do you trust me, Eva?"

Swallowing past the lump in her throat she turned to the side and told him her answer. "Yes."

"Good." His finger slid inside her ass. He took his time, and the bite of pain had her groaning. "Easy. Don't move. It'll hurt to start."

"I don't like pain."

"This is good pain."

And it was. Her pussy was burning up, and the arousal was clawing away making it hard for her to simply lie there on the bed and wait for him to finish with her.

"That's it," he said. His voice sounded soothing

to her. "Take my cock, and if you're a good girl I'll fuck that tight, hot ass."

Whimpering, she watched him in the mirror slide a second finger inside her. It was entirely erotic, explicit, and she didn't know if she'd ever survive such a possession. Tiny consumed her entire body with his. There was not a part of her left unturned in his hard loving.

Achingly slowly he withdrew from her pussy with only the tip of him inside her. She missed him and wanted him back.

"I can't wait any longer." His fingers left her ass to return to her hips. Tiny pounded inside her hard and fast, refusing to let up. His hands were bruising where he held her. She went on her arms thrusting back against him.

His hands moved from her hips around to her stomach, drawing her up against his body. Fingers tweaked her nipples as another hand slid down to cup her mound.

"I want to feel you come on my dick," Tiny said, growling against her neck. "Fuck." He shouted the curse, which echoed off the walls. Crying out, she let herself go feeling her orgasm rage through her.

Turning her onto her back, Tiny placed her in the center of the bed. He was still hard as rock. She couldn't believe the stamina of the man.

Opening her thighs wide, Tiny fisted his shaft before sliding back inside. She should have been embarrassed by how easily he stroked inside her.

"I love how wet you are for me." He took her hands within his, locking their fingers together. Tiny pressed them to the bed beside her head. She stared into his eyes as he tenderly started to make love to her. Leaning down he claimed her lips, plunging his tongue into her mouth. She moaned, opening her lips to receive him.

"I fucking love you," he said, biting down on her bottom lip. "I'll never grow tired of this. You're mine."

She didn't know how long they lay on the bed as it felt like a lifetime to her. In his arms with his cock inside her and all of his attention focused on her Eva knew she could never walk away from him. Her path was melded with his.

****

Tiny pushed inside her feeling the beginning of his orgasm. He wouldn't close his eyes. More than anything he wanted to watch her come apart. Holding onto her hands he stared at the woman he loved with all of his heart. She took every part of him and never once let him get away with shit. Evangeline Walker was his soul mate. He felt it deep into his core.

Pressing inside her one final time his cum erupted, filling her body with his seed. He closed his eyes, and memories of Eva swamped him. The seconds that passed were precious to him, and yet he worshipped every memory. The day Tate graduated and Eva stood by his side even though he was covered in dirt and grease from working. The times he'd gotten home from the club and she'd been there with a warm meal and smile. Even the times he got home after fucking a woman who wasn't her and she'd screamed and raged at him.

No, Eva was not a weak-willed woman. She was what he needed in a woman. When he needed to be taken care of and not have shit, Eva gave it to him. When he needed a kick up the ass, she gave it to him with equal measure. She made him earn her respect and attention. No other woman had made him fight for a crumb whereas Eva made him fight for a chance to be with her.

He loved her with his whole heart, and he would

sacrifice everything to keep her safe. His club meant the world to him, but Eva was his sanity.

Collapsing against her he basked in her scent and the feel of her pussy fluttering around his length.

"Tiny, baby, you're squashing me," Eva said, coughing.

Moving to her side, Tiny stayed inside her not wanting to leave the warmth of her body. Releasing her hand, he leaned on one of his hands, and he caressed her face with the other.

"Is it me, or did Tiny, the deadly leader of The Skulls, just make love to me?" she asked, smiling.

Leaning down, he captured her lips and smiled. "Shh, don't tell anyone. I've got a reputation to protect."

"I can only imagine what men would think of a guy who makes love and not fucks."

"Hey, I fucked your brains out, and I was being considerate to you, baby. I don't want you all hurt." Kissing her again, he chuckled at her moan. Her cunt tightened around his dick.

Her fingers stroked up and down his arm. Sighing, he'd never felt so complete before in his life.

Taking hold of one of her hands, he pressed a kiss to the finger that wore his band. "My ring looks good on you."

"Will you be willing to wear a ring from me?" she asked, smirking.

"Baby, I'll wear anything you give me with pride."

She giggled as he rubbed his nose against hers. "You're just a big cuddly teddy bear."

Laughing, he locked their fingers together still with his head resting in his free hand. All the worries of the last forty-eight hours melted away. "Only with you, and don't forget I can still bite." He bit down on her nipple for good measure.

Her giggling turned into a moan. He felt her pussy ripple around him as he tortured her bud.

"I'll get you a ring," Eva said as he released her bud. Her hand tightened around his. "I need to make sure all those women swarming around you know you're mine."

He nodded, thinking about Fort Wills. Tiny wondered what mess he would find when he returned. The compound was burned to the ground.

"Just to warn you when I'm your woman I won't be nice to the other bitches. They try it on with you, and they'll answer to me. No cheating, no screwing around on me, Tiny."

"I'm all yours." He squeezed her hand again hoping she got the message.

Her smile dropped. "What are you thinking about?"

"Nothing, baby."

"You don't get to do that anymore. I'm not going to be pushed aside. When you're worrying about something, share it with me. I'll carry the burden with you." She didn't pull away even though he expected her to.

"I'm thinking about my men and the club."

"Tate told me Sandy burnt it down to the ground," Eva said.

"Yeah, Stink got the order to pass on the failsafe."

"Do you mind me asking why?" She lifted their hands in the air. "Why burn your compound to the ground? Why create a failsafe?"

"To protect the club and the men. Details about our contracts, our runs, and even my men were locked up tight in that fucking compound. We all agreed that nothing could be left to someone else stumbling on shit. Disposing of all evidence is the only way to go. With Snitch back, he's going to go after the club and anyone associated with my men." Tiny sighed, seeing the ambush once again in his mind. Lash, Nash, Murphy, and Zero all falling. They were all his men, and yet he'd ignored his unease and just taken the job anyway.

"How will you know they're alive?" Eva asked. "You know Stink and Killer are alive, but what about the others?"

"They know to get in contact with Alex. He'll round them up, and then we'll know when to hit out." Tiny didn't like how slowly his men were coming back to him. Last time he checked none of them had heard from Lash, Nash, or Murphy.

"Snitch has an issue, and he's going to try to take Fort Wills to get revenge on you." Eva wasn't asking a question.

"Yeah, Killer's going to protect Tate. She won't leave town, which just shows what a pain in the ass she is. I can't force her to leave. She's staying in case Murphy shows up, stubborn fucking bitch. Killer's there, so I'm not too concerned. I know him, and he'll protect all of the women." He couldn't force his daughter to leave town when he wasn't even there to make sure she did as she was told. "Strong willed girl."

Eva chuckled. "She takes after her father."

"Whatever. She should learn to do as she's told," Tiny said, getting angry.

"Easy, Killer will protect her, and I imagine the town will do whatever they can to keep themselves safe. They'll know everything you've done for them now."

He nodded, wishing he could believe her words. "Or I'll find out how much they hate having a biker group keeping order."

"If this man is as bad as you say he is then I don't doubt their loyalty to you."

Tiny hated the way the mood was going. Pulling out of her body, he grabbed a robe, wrapping it around him. "I'm going to go and check on Alex. He likes to keep everything to himself."

"Fine, go and do your leader thing. I'm going to watch a movie or get some sleep. It has been a long couple of weeks."

Moving away from the bed, Tiny got to the doorway. "What did your father say about my proposal?" he asked, turning back to her.

She groaned, her face going into the pillow. Her rounded ass called to him, but he stayed still.

"Come on, it can't be that bad." Leaning against the wall, he folded his arms across his chest.

"He doesn't want you taking over for his men. Gavin is a more ideal solution to him," Eva said.

Tiny hated the sound of Gavin and her father more and more. He'd not gotten to know the other man, but he clearly loved his daughter, even if he hadn't followed her when she left.

"You're my woman. You wear my ring," he said.

"I know that. I kneed Gavin in the balls when he told me you were too old for me."

Annoyed, Tiny tensed up. He would like to show this fucking Gavin who was fucking old and not.

"Good girl, baby. I'll be back. Don't disappear on me." He spun on his heel and headed out of the room. Several guards were posted outside of his door. They gave him a nod as he closed the door.

"Make sure she doesn't leave this room and no one enters besides me," he said.

"Of course, Tiny," the guard said, answering him.

Leaving the hallway he went into the elevator and

punched for the third floor where he knew Alex set up his business. If there was ever a raid or a burglary, Alex didn't like to be obvious in his choice of storage.

"You've gotten away already? I figured I wouldn't see you for a day at least."

"I've got my men to worry about," Tiny said, sitting down opposite his former brother-in-law. "Have any of them gotten in touch?"

Alex handed him a piece of paper. "Zero is recuperating. He's not given me his location, but he's desperate to get the bastards for hurting him."

Tiny listened as Alex went down the list of men who had gotten in touch. "You've still not heard anything from Lash, Nash, and Murphy?"

"No. I'm making calls to local hospitals asking for Nigel and Edward. They'll use their real names."

"What about Murphy? Any news at hospitals for him?" He couldn't return home to take back his town without his daughter's man. She was pregnant, and anything could make that pregnancy go wrong. He couldn't risk hurting his daughter any more than he already had.

"Nothing, Tiny. I can't find him. Killer told me he saw Murphy's bike explode."

"Murphy is a good rider. He can't be dead."

Staring at Alex, he saw the somber expression on his face. "You may have to consider the fact he could be dead."

Standing up, Tiny stormed toward the window staring out over the Vegas landscape. "I can't do that."

"Tiny, be reasonable."

"Murphy is Tate's husband. They're expecting their first baby. I can't go back without bringing him with me." Tiny pressed his palm to the window, feeling the panic start to claw up inside him.

"Then for your sake, I hope he's alive. You don't want to wait around while Snitch gets any stronger."

Tiny stayed in his position staring out of the window. *Murphy, where the fuck are you?*
****

"What are we waiting for?" Kelsey asked, coming out of the bedroom. Sophia, Angel, and Tate were staying with them in the small apartment. Killer hadn't allowed the women to leave once he'd spoken to Tiny. His mission was to keep all of them safe.

Staring out of the window, Killer wished he knew what the hell was going on. The women were crying, then reasoning with each other. None of them knew the danger each of their men had faced on the road.

"You're not waiting for anything." He checked his gun for the tenth time.

"You're waiting for something though." Kelsey sat opposite him. He was struck by her cherry blonde hair. Killer didn't even care that the color came out of a box. He'd seen Tate dye her hair before.

"The men who attacked were not doing it for fun." He rubbed a hand down his face feeling tired from everything that had happened. His side hurt from the grazed bullet. Kelsey was taking care of him though, and he felt good just by being in her presence. "They wanted something, and with Sandy stopping by with shit from the compound's safe, Tiny knows they want it as well."

"Do you think they're coming to town?"

He'd burned his cut around the back of the apartments. Alex advised he cut all visible ties with the club until Tiny said further.

"Yeah, they're coming to town. I'm simply waiting for them to arrive."

Kelsey let out a shaky breath and turned away. "I'll make a drink."

"Coffee, please." He didn't watch her walk away. Whenever he stared at her shapely ass Killer wanted her.

Ten minutes later he held the coffee in his hand as the rumble of bikes sounded close by. Staring out of the window he recognized the bikes as they passed by. "Here we go," Killer said. Grabbing Tate's cell phone he dialed Alex's number.

"Yes?" Alex asked.

"They're here."

Chapter Eleven

Snitch climbed off his bike inhaling the scent of Fort Wills. He was home, and The Skulls were fucking gone. The compound was down to the ground, but he didn't give a shit. The town was now his own. His men climbed off the bike, Battle and Scars flanking his side.

"We did it, Snitch. We're back in your town," Scars said.

Smiling, he looked up and down the street that was now his own. The sound of sirens alerted him to the presence of the law. They were all going to be in fucking shock. Clicking his knuckles, he tensed up waiting for the brawl about to happen. No one ever told him what to do and got away with it.

"Boys, we're going to have a showdown. Let's show these good people how it's fucking done." Snitch couldn't believe all it had taken was luring The Skulls out of town. Finding Ned had been a stroke of genius, and luring The Skulls out to a planned run was perfection. Like always, patience meant fucking perfect. He wondered what had distracted Tiny enough to take the run with the planned route. He'd put money it would have to do with that fucking slut he was panting after.

Like so many fucking men, Tiny got his dick locked on one fucking woman.

The cars came to a stop in front of him and his men. Glancing behind him he saw the men grabbing their crowbars and guns ready to rain down hell.

"Sir, I'm going to have to ask you to leave," the man dressed in a cop uniform said coming closer. He looked nervous, and Snitch laughed.

"Are you going to be the one to get rid of me?" Snitch asked, stepping closer. Scars pressed a crowbar to his hand behind his back.

"With all due respect, you're not welcome here." The man stood his ground.

Snitch was impressed. Most men ran from him when he started advancing closer.

"I'm not going anywhere." Swinging the crowbar around, he slammed the metal against the man's face. "And you're not going to get rid of me."

The cops looked petrified. Tiny really had become the law in Fort Wills. Snitch couldn't help but be impressed. The cop went down as he held the crowbar by his side. Snitch loved the feel of breaking bones. Another cop ran at him, and he used his fist, slamming his knuckles into the face, loving the feel of flesh on flesh. The fight ensued, each cop trying to take them on. Snitch laughed as over and over again he lashed out taking back his town. Tiny had taken this away from him, and if the fucking bastard wasn't dead then he'd have the pleasure of hunting him down and killing him.

Twenty minutes later the cops were on the ground, moaning, whimpering and clutching their injuries. He imagined the folks were watching him from their apartment windows.

"I want you to all listen up," Snitch said, yelling into the night. He threw the crowbar to the floor beside him. "The Skulls are all fucking dead. Your town is no longer theirs, and they will not be coming to your rescue. They're dead."

The joy filled him at the news.

"From now on, you'll be getting your orders from us." Pulling the gun out of his pocket he aimed it at the first man's head. "Anyone who doesn't and tries to defy me will get this." He shot the man in the head.

It was time for Fort Wills to know who they were dealing with.
****

Tiny cursed, throwing the cell phone Alex handed to him against the opposite wall. "Getting angry at phones is not going to be the answer to our problems," Alex said.

"Snitch has killed one of the people I swore to fucking protect." Tiny slammed his fist into the wall. The pain did nothing to ease his anger or the feeling of deep seated hatred he felt for the man of his past.

"You can't do anything about him, Tiny. You've got no choice but to bide your time and hope the others call soon. There's nothing else we can do other than hope he doesn't go after Tate." Alex sat forward trying to reason with him.

"She's vulnerable, Alex. My daughter, my flesh and blood, is within the same town that fucking lunatic is. I know Snitch. He'll hunt her down and fucking destroy her." Tiny knew Snitch would do a hell of a lot more than simply hurt her. Snitch would break her down, rape her, beat her, make her wish for death long before he gave it to her.

"Killer will never let anything happen to her. He's loyal, and we've got to find Murphy. Turning up without him will ruin her far more. She loves that boy, and no matter what I tell her, she won't fucking budge. You really should have taught her to do as she was told growing up."

"She won't leave. I've begged her, and so has Eva. She's staying in case her man shows up. She's too much of a fucking brat. Fucking boy better show up soon."

Tiny couldn't believe he was thinking of Murphy as a boy. Still, compared to him, Murphy *was* nothing but a boy.

"Fine, give me the phone. I'll call Killer back," Tiny said. He sat beside Alex as the other man dialed the number.

Eva. He needed to think of his woman to get him through the painful moments.

"My doctor will be by to have a look at your wounds," Alex said as he got Killer on the phone. He'd not thought about the pain since the news of Snitch's return to fucking Fort Wills. Tiny knew in that instant he should have done more to hunt the bastard down and kill him years ago.

"Hello, boss, I wish I could give you some good news," Killer said.

"Is Tate with you?" he asked, rubbing his temples. He felt the stirrings of a headache begin.

"She's in the other bedroom. They all fucking screamed. I had to turn the lights off and shut the blinds. I don't want to draw attention to the apartment. Snitch doesn't look like a man you want to get in a dispute with."

"No, he's not. I need you to promise me you'll keep Tate safe. If you can convince her to leave then do it. I want her out of harm's way."

"What about Murphy?" Killer asked.

"Still no word. Keep her safe for me. I'm sorry to put you in this position." Tiny looked up at the red headed doctor as she walked in.

"Boss, no worries. I've got a reason to stick around if you know what I mean." Tiny knew the answer, Kelsey.

"Good. Keep the women safe, and I'll keep you updated."

"If you want my advice, boss, hurry. This guy is unstable, and he's going to start hunting in the morning. I've told Kelsey she can't go out to work. Something tells me these men are not going to care about the women who refuse them."

Tiny agreed with him. "Stay close to the phone, and do not let my daughter out of your sight. If anything happens I'll end you, understand?"

"Boss, if anything happens to these women, I'll end myself."

The call was disconnected as the red head went to her knees before him. She pushed his robe out of the way to assess the bandages. "How is the pain?"

"Not bad for those special pills you gave me," he said.

She sported a wedding ring, and he felt even more comfortable in her company. "You're married?"

"Five years now. Marrying him was the best thing I ever did. I love him so damn much." She was smiling as she talked.

"Where did you go for your honeymoon?" he asked.

"The Caribbean. It was beautiful. The heat, the food, the setting, it was perfect. Are you thinking of getting married?" She gently removed the bandage. "You were incredibly lucky."

"I was wearing my gear. I'm a lot of things, Red, but I'm not a fucking idiot."

She chuckled.

"I'm engaged. I've been married before, and it didn't end well."

"Divorce?"

"No, she died of cancer. Left me with a kid and a hatred of marriage. We married quickly when we didn't even really know each other. I thought we were good together, and at times we were, but we weren't always compatible, which made for some really hard times. Shit, I shouldn't be telling you this shit."

"I'm a doctor. It's my job to be told things."

"Still, marriage is a gamble no matter what. I just

didn't get the big bonus in the end."

"I'm sorry," Red said.

"Don't be. I finally found the woman for me." He waited for her to finish with his bandages.

"You're healing nicely. Your protective clothing kept most of the damage at bay. If you hadn't been wearing them you could have lost a leg by now." Red got up, taking her rubber gloves off. She snapped her case closed and turned to him. "Keep changing the bandages, press on the ointment, and in a week try to keep the wound clear to give it time to heal. I don't see any other problem with your condition."

"Thanks, Red. I appreciate you coming here to look after me."

"Take care, Tiny. I'll give Alex my bill."

For several minutes he sat on the sofa trying to relax. His woman was upstairs, probably asleep and waiting for his attention.

"If she wasn't married she'd be in my bed so fucking fast. I bet she has a nice tight pussy to drown yourself in," Alex said, walking back into the room.

"We square for the bill?" Tiny asked.

"Yeah. After I sent you into a fucking trap, it's the least I can do. "

"I'm going back to Eva." Tiny stood ready to leave.

"I am sorry," Alex said, following him out to the door.

"What about?" Tiny asked, holding onto the door handle then turning back to look at the other man.

"I would never have gotten you involved or put you and The Skulls in danger. You're my brother, Tiny. We're not related by blood or by relation, but to me, you're my brother."

"I know, man, I know. I suggest you get fucking

Ned Walker and that punk Gavin. See if they had anything to do with my set up."

"What if no one had anything to do with it?" Alex asked.

"Then Snitch is a sneaky bastard to get past your defenses, and you better make sure it doesn't happen again. People dying is bad for fucking business."

Closing the door behind him, Tiny made his way upstairs to his woman. The guard nodded at him. Tiny nodded back and entered his room. The sound of the television playing echoed throughout the whole room. Going to the bedroom, he saw Eva passed out across the base of the bed. She wore her robe, which had opened up to her waist. He got a tempting view of her mound. His mouth watered, remembering the taste of her. Going to the bedside drawer, he pulled out a tube of lube and a condom.

Tiny needed inside her, and if he got a chance to sample her tight ass then he was happy about that.

In the morning he'd deal with Ned and Gavin. After that he was getting his men together, and he needed to come up with a plan to take on Fort Wills. Snitch had done his work on all of the men. There was no way Tiny could just drive back into town shooting the place up. He would never risk the lives of innocent people, and with Snitch involved, innocent people always ended up dead. Removing his robe, he climbed in behind her. Untying her belt, he opened her gown, giving him enough room to caress her breast before going down to her stomach. She moaned, rubbing against him.

"Come on, baby, wake up for me."

He slipped his fingers down to stroke her pussy. She was slick to the touch. He moaned as he slid two fingers easily inside her.

"So fucking juicy, wake up, baby. I want to fuck

you."

She moaned. "Tiny, I was sleeping."

"And now you're not." Tugging the robe out of his way, he lifted her leg in the air and pressed his hard cock to her entrance. Her pussy wanted him, swallowing him up as he slid deep inside her.

Turning her head to claim her lips, he kissed her muffling her cries of pleasure.

"Where were you?" she asked.

Releasing her lips, he sucked onto her neck.

"Business. We'll talk after. First I have to fuck you."

He slammed inside her loving the feel of her cunt rippling around him. Tiny would die a happy man with her heat surrounding him.

"Tiny," she said, chanting his name over and over again.

"Yeah, baby, say my name. Beg for it, and I'll give you everything you fucking need." Pounding her pussy, he sucked at her neck, marking her as his own. When he met that fucking asshole who wanted her, Tiny wanted him to know who Eva belonged to.

The sounds of moaning drew his attention to the screen. "Were you watching porn?"

"I didn't know you were going to be so long," Eva said. "I got bored with waiting for you."

"Did you play with my pussy?" he asked, getting turned on at the thought of what he missed.

"Yes."

Pulling out of her tight heat, he turned on the light and swiftly moved her into the center of the bed. "You're going to make me beg for it now, aren't you?" she asked.

"No, I'm going to take that ass, and I'm going to watch you play with your cunt while I do." Grabbing the condom where he left it, he ripped into the foil packet and slid the latex over his erection. Leaning over her, he grabbed some pillows and placed them under her hips making it possible for him to claim her ass as she played with herself. Her curvy body looked ready for a nice hard fucking.

With the tube of lube, he opened the cap and squirted some lube onto his fingers before sliding his coated fingers to her puckered ass. "I'm going to get you nice and wet." He slapped her hand away as she went to play with her clit.

"No, you wait for me to tell you when to play."

She smiled. "Yes, Sir."

He glared at her, but she simply smiled wider at him. Shaking his head, he coated her anus with plenty of lube before coating his fingers again to stroke inside her tight ass.

"Relax as I push this into you. This is going to make it easy for me to claim your fucking ass," he said.

Pushing against her tight ring of muscles, Tiny kept up the pressure determined to get inside her. She relaxed giving him the ease to slide his fingers into her ass.

"That wasn't so hard, was it?" he asked.

"It's easy for you to say. You don't have a finger up your ass." He tutted at her anger then chuckled.

"I'll be making it worth your while. You'll be begging for my cock in your ass," he said.

She growled in frustration. He worked her ass open making sure there was plenty of lube to slicken her for his entry. When he was satisfied he rubbed more lube around his latex-covered cock.

"I'm going to take you slow. You'll do as you're told, and only when I say will you start to play with yourself."

"You're bossy," she said, sticking her tongue out.

"Baby, I'm the fucking boss, so you'll do as I say."

He aligned the head of his cock against her ass. She stopped speaking as he pressed the tip against her puckered entrance. "If I knew taking your ass would shut you up I'd have taken you there months ago."

Eva didn't say anything. Her hands were fisted in the blanket on either side of her.

"Got nothing to say? No wisecrack or insult?"

"Stop it, Tiny," she said, blowing out a breath.

The teasing left him as he pushed the tip inside her ass. Her tight muscles eased as he forged his way inside.

She reached out, ordering him to stop. Her hands covered his where he held her legs.

"What's the matter?" he asked.

"It … feels … strange."

"Good or bad?" If she didn't like it he wasn't going to force her the rest of the way. He had hoped she would start to like what he was doing to her.

****

Eva gasped as an explosion of pleasure consumed her taking control of her senses. She never thought it was possible to love a man inside her ass. Tiny had stopped when she asked him to, and she stared up into his eyes to see the love shining down on her.

She remembered that he asked her question. "Good, it's good."

"Can I move?"

"Yes," she said, breathing a sigh of relief. He slid inside her another inch, teasing her with the promise of more.

"I'm going to fill your ass. Do you feel me?"

"Yes." She wanted him to fill her ass. To take whatever he wanted from her body. The pleasure and her body were his for the taking.

His hands moved to her hips, gripping her flesh. Another inch was inside her, and she couldn't handle it anymore. She had to feel all of him inside her.

"Please, Tiny, fuck me."

"I told you, you'd be begging me to fuck you."

She didn't like the satisfaction on his face, but there was nothing for her to do. Tiny was right. The pain and pleasure mixed from his taking her ass were indescribable. Her pussy felt on fire, and her arousal was slick.

"I can see how turned on you're getting, baby. You're loving me in your ass just like I love being there."

She didn't say another word as he took full possession of her body, thrusting into her ass until the hilt. There was nowhere else for him to go. She screamed as he tensed, sending the next inch in deep.

"That's it, baby. You've got me all."

Letting out a breath, Eva stared up at him. His cock pulsed inside her ass, and she felt every jerk of his shaft.

"Touch yourself now." She moved her hand between her thighs. "Don't close your thighs. I want to watch. Your cunt is leaking our cum, Eva. I can see us together."

"You've never worn a condom with me before," she said.

"I'm taking your ass, and I'd rather be safe than sorry."

Eva wasn't questioning him. They could be pregnant, and she wouldn't even know. Her body was aflame with all that he was.

"Slide your fingers inside."

She pressed a finger into her cunt, feeling the

penetration combined with the cock up her ass. Eva had never been so turned on. When she thought sex couldn't get any better, Tiny had a way of making it even more explosive than she could ever imagine.

"Add another finger. That juicy pussy can take so much more." She wished it was his fingers pressing inside her, instead of her own. His fingers were rougher and larger. Eva knew she would never get the satisfaction with her hands.

"Another," he said, ordering her. His voice was hard and firm. She felt herself getting turned on by his rough commands. He was the man in charge, and she loved him for it.

She added a third finger to her pussy, sliding her digits inside. Eva felt stretched from her hands. Licking her lips, she couldn't look away as Tiny watched her hands.

He moved her hand away. Tiny hadn't moved, and his cock was like a rock hard brand inside her ass. Eva gasped as three of his fingers fucked inside her. Crying out, she tightened around his cock and fingers as he fucked her.

"So wet and tight."

Tiny turned his fingers, stroking inside her over her G-spot. She splintered apart, screaming her orgasm as he continued to caress the spot inside her that took away every sense of control.

"Now, touch your clit. I want to see you stroke your pussy and bring yourself to orgasm."

"I can't orgasm again."

"Baby, if you can't have multiple orgasms then I'm doing something wrong."

His confidence made her tense. This man was a fucking sex machine. There was no denying him.

He eased out of her ass slowly before sliding back

inside. She stroked her clit, feeling the hard nub swell against her fingers.

"I'm fucking your ass, Eva," he said.

She felt him. His hard cock, slick with lube, fucked her ass.

"You're dripping wet." One of his hands moved from her hip to slide through her cunt. He slid inside her in time with the thrusts of his cock. "I'll buy you a dildo, and I'll be inside your ass as I fuck your cunt with the fake cock."

She glided her fingers down to mix with his inside her. Together they worked inside her cunt, her arousal slick enough for both of them. Easing out, she stroked her clit feeling the first building of arousal. She didn't think it was possible to experience another orgasm so soon after her last one. Her body was on fire once again begging for release.

"Yeah, baby, I feel the difference inside you. You're going to come over my fingers, and I'll feel your tight ass getting ready to take my cum."

Eva increased her strokes over her clit. She felt sensitive all over. The rough pads of Tiny's fingers at her hips made her already sensitive flesh feeling like it was burning. She loved his rough hands and wouldn't change the way he made her feel for the world.

"Come for me, Eva."

As if her body was commanded by his words alone, Eva found her release. Crying out, she stroked her clit through her orgasm. Closing her eyes, she felt taken over by love and lust.

He rode her ass through the orgasm. His fingers moved away from her as she came out of her orgasm. "That's it, baby. Now it's my turn."

Hands on her hips, Tiny showed her what it really meant to be owned by a Skull. He fucked her hard, yet gently, each thrust designed to purposefully bring her greater pleasure. "So fucking tight and hot. Never letting you go. You're all mine."

"Yes, Tiny. I'm yours," she said, thrusting back against him. She gripped his thighs wanting to feel his release inside her.

"Love you so fucking much. My woman, my pussy, my fucking ass."

Eva wasn't going to argue with him. She'd been his for a long time now. It was only him and his actions that had kept them apart.

"I love you," she said.

He fucked her hard for five more thrusts. Tiny growled as his cock jerked in her ass. She felt his shaft pump with seed into the latex. Within seconds his cock started to ease, going flaccid within her. He collapsed on top of her still in her ass.

"I've died and gone to fucking heaven," he said, muttering the words against her neck.

Chuckling, she caressed his back, loving the weight of him. "If you're in heaven then you better watch your language."

"Then I'm in hell that feels like heaven."

Smiling, she ran her hands all over his body, touching what she now owned herself.

"I love you, Tiny," she said, kissing his cheek.

He moved over her, resting his hands either side of her head. "I love you, too, baby." Looking down their bodies, he grunted before returning to look at her. "Now I've got to get you cleaned up."

"I don't want to be cleaned up. I want to stay here."

"I wouldn't be a very good husband if I didn't clean up my mess." He climbed off her, withdrawing from her ass, taking great care as he did.

Eva cried out as he picked her up, carrying her back into the bathroom. She felt so tired and sluggish, not that she needed to worry about doing anything. Tiny took care of her in the only way he knew how, by doing everything himself.

He ran her a bath then eased her back inside.

"Are you coming in with me?" she asked.

"I can't. I've got my leg," he said, pointing at the bandages down one side.

She moaned, sitting back against the tub.

"I'll clean you, and we'll have more time for each other."

Eva didn't argue. She watched him clean himself up by the sink before he turned back to her. He was frowning, and she knew he was worrying.

"What did Alex have to say?" she asked, knowing in her heart only club problems could put that expression on his face.

"There's still no word from Murphy or Lash and Nash."

He ran a hand down his face.

"You don't think they're dead, do you?" she asked, concerned for the other men.

"I don't know. Killer's last sight of Murphy was his fucking bike."

Eva thought about Tate. The other woman was a hard assed woman, but the death of Murphy could send her spiraling with no way out from the hell she'd create for herself. Tiny gave her a list of the men who'd gotten in touch. Most of them were injured but being treated. Zero was with a family friend or something. The only three men who'd not been in contact were the three men with wives waiting for them.

"I can't come back without my daughter's man. I hate Murphy because I know he's screwing my daughter, but she loves him and he loves her. I can't come between that, and I cannot go home without him."

"Every father hates the men in their daughter's life." She didn't mention Gavin as her father seemed to like him.

She listened as he explained everything that had happened since he left her. Snitch was in Fort Wills, and there was nothing Tiny could do until he called Devil and then rounded up the men. So far he'd found Time and Gunn hadn't made it. Whizz had called to tell him the news. The men had suffered severe burns and blood loss. Tiny hated the news. All of his men meant something to him, but he couldn't spend the time dwelling on it. They would get their town back, and Tiny would put Snitch in the ground once and for all.

After he washed her, she took a robe and wrapped it around herself. She cupped his face, staring into his eyes. "I love you, Tiny. There's time for us later. I'll be your wife and stand by your side, but we can't sit around, screwing when your men need you."

"What do you suggest?" he asked.

Taking his hand, she led him into the bedroom. Grabbing her cell phone, she pointed to where the room's phone lay beside the bed. "I'll get the directory and start making calls to local hospitals and stations. You call Devil and start to come up with a plan."

"Why?"

"Because the people of Fort Wills need you, and this bastard needs to be put in the ground."

Picking up the cell phone, she dialed the first hospital and started to ask around for the men. She wouldn't give up until she saw the dead bodies of Murphy, Lash, and Nash with her own two eyes.

Chapter Twelve

Killer sat in the coffee shop, watching the bikers beat up a helpless citizen. Tensing in his seat, he tried not to make his presence known. The owner of the shop had seated him in the corner near where he could see the action but not be spotted by the men hurting his town. Fort Wills hadn't started out being his town, but he was part of it now.

The man leaning against the cop car was the leader. He'd heard the men refer to him as Snitch. Killer had left the women at the apartment armed with a gun. He needed to check out what was going on. Waiting in the apartment expecting the men to come looking for either him or Tate was driving him crazy.

"You're safe here," the owner, Langnor, said, pouring him some coffee. Glancing up at the man, Killer was surprised to see the compassion in his face.

"Do you know who he is?" Killer asked.

"Yeah, I recognize him. He's the reason we trust Tiny and The Skulls. Bad fucking sort and I hope you guys are ready to put him in the fucking ground for good this time." The owner looked angrily at the other man. "Last time he was in Fort Wills, he killed my brother. I love this town and consider myself a placid person. Seeing him has reminded me of all the hatred I have for him and his sort."

"Is that sort like me and Tiny?" Killer asked, ready to swipe the bastard for any bad word said about Tiny.

"No. You guys are decent and do your best to keep this town safe. If they come our way, head out the back. No one will stop you, and I'll make sure your identity is protected."

Killer nodded. He believed if Snitch wanted to

get him, he already knew what all The Skulls looked like.

Snitch pulled away from the car. "Now, all I want to know is where Tate is. Tiny's daughter. You all know the fat bitch. I want her, and all this pain goes away." Someone had opened the door, and they all paused as Snitch mentioned Tate's name.

Everyone knew if they gave up Tate, they'd have to face Tiny's wrath.

"I don't know, man," the guy who was being beaten said. Snitch punched him again in the face. The unknown man went down where Snitch proceeded to kick the man with his boots. Killer knew the man would die if no one stopped it. The gun in his pocket burned.

"Do you have a window I could use?" Killer asked. He wasn't going to sit back watching these fuckers take one of his men. It was time for him to even the score.

Langnor pointed upstairs. Nodding his head, Killer gave him a warning that things were going to get ugly and to keep kids' eyes away.

Heading upstairs, Killer knew he could be sent to his death for what he was about to do. His only hope would be the shock all the men experienced as he took out one of their own.

One of the windows was partially open. Pulling out his gun, he checked to make sure everything was safe and sat down looking at the men. The one closest to Snitch was his safest bet.

Remember, Killer, protect, serve, and stay safe.

Breathing out, Killer allowed all of his calm and stillness to build inside him. Everything around him went silent as he lined up the shot. He had the perfect head shot.

One ... two ... three. Killer fired, and the man went down. During the ensuing silence, he watched as the men took cover.

"Scars?" Snitch asked. The man's voice was loud enough for Killer to hear.

"He's dead, Snitch. Through the fucking head."

Killer heard all of them talking. At the sound of a gun going off, he looked out of the window to see Snitch had shot the man on the floor through the head.

"I'm warning you all now, if you're protecting a Skull or any of the whores then you'll die just like them."

The warning was noted. Pulling out Kelsey's cell phone, Killer dialed Alex's number. "You're going to need to start rounding up the men. Snitch is after the women and any Skulls he didn't kill. It's only a matter of time before he fucks everyone up."

He'd given them some time. Snitch looked like the kind of man to mourn his dead, especially with how sad he looked at the fallen man. It was a risk Killer had to take, and he'd do it again in a heartbeat. Killer doubted they'd get a lot of time before he started picking off the people of Fort Wills. Whatever Tiny had done to Snitch had left him in need of vengeance. Killer hadn't seen anyone intent on causing this much damage, not even The Lions.

Come on, Tiny. Come and save our fucking asses.
****

Tiny held Eva's hand as he stared across the desk at Ned Walker and the asshole Gavin. He didn't care if Gavin was an upstanding citizen. The other man had designs on his woman, and that he didn't fucking accept.

"What the fuck are you accusing me of?" Ned Walker asked.

On the other side of Eva sat Alex. Their guards were outside keeping the fighters at bay. Tiny wasn't under any illusions that the fighters wouldn't attack. He imagined Ned brought up the best and dirtiest fighters he could.

"It's simple, Ned. You're a family man, and you knew Eva was in Fort Wills. Did you arrange for The Darkness or more importantly, Snitch, to attack The Skulls?" Alex asked.

Alex was cool, calm, and collected. Tiny wondered if his friend even knew how to get angry. He wouldn't ever see if Alex was as hard as they said. The man had a reputation that Tiny respected. No one got to own a reputable casino without being a hard nut first. Alex had guards who were loyal and took care of him.

"Who the fuck do you think you're talking to, boy?" Ned stood, slamming the chair back.

"Dad," Eva said. Her grip tightened in his hand.

He held her hand, giving her the strength from his own.

"No, Eva, you're my fucking daughter, but no one comes into my place of business and accuses me of being fucking dirty." Tiny was inclined to believe Ned was innocent. "I've been doing business a lot longer than you've been born, Eva. No one makes me become dirty to get you home. You're old enough to know when you want to come home. I'm not the one to stop you or control you."

"With all due respect, I took your fucking order, and my men, the men I've come to know like fucking brothers were attacked. We can't find three of the fuckers, and you're starting to piss me off. Are you fucking dirty?" Alex asked, still keeping his cool.

Tiny watched the other man stand, leaning against the desk, getting into Ned's face without even looking threatening.

"Get out!" Gavin said, yelling.

"Shut your fucking mouth. This has nothing to do with you." Tiny stood, releasing Eva's hand. He was ready to wipe Gavin's face off. The jealousy he felt toward the other man was threatening to drown him. Moving Alex out of the way, Tiny focused his attention on Ned. "You're a father. I get your need to protect our daughter. I love Eva with my whole heart, and no, I didn't take care of her the way she deserved but I can make that up now." He stopped to glance at Eva. She was smiling at him, which he loved even though their life was going to get tense in the coming days.

He'd called Devil, who was rounding up his men to get the revenge they all wanted. Snitch had fucked them over, and he'd learned on the phone that Snitch was responsible for killing Devil's sister. There was so much bad shit among them all. Tiny was going to end the bastard, and he was going to start fresh. No more past and no more bad shit coming to his men or his town.

"I love my daughter, and her man is missing. He could be dead. I will have to face *my* little girl and tell her that I failed. I was responsible for putting her man in the ground." Ned hadn't spoken a word but was glaring at him. "When she gets over the pain I know my daughter, and she's going to ask for the head of the man who caused her man to be dead." Letting the threat sink in, Tiny turned to look at Gavin. "I'll bring my baby all of their heads. I need to know if you're added to the list because the moment my little girl cries, I'll kill anyone I think is responsible."

Easing back into his chair, he watched as Ned sat back down looking at his girl.

"I get your threat, and I can promise you that I had nothing to do with the attack. If I wanted you taken care of I'd see to it, Tiny." Ned looked at Eva. "I love *my* little girl, but I wouldn't be dirty to get her back."

He watched Ned turn and open the safe. "I got a call two weeks ago. A new buyer wanted a shipment of coke. He was looking to distribute, and once he got settled the money would be flowing." Ned handed over the file. "This is who I dealt with. I don't make connections without having back up. I've never been to Fort Wills other than to see my daughter. I don't know your past, Tiny."

Taking the file, Tiny looked down at Snitch. The man was a lot older, but it was Snitch.

"That's him. He's the one I, Mikey, and Devil rode out of town over twenty years ago."

Handing the file back, Tiny felt the anger rolling over him. "He's been watching us for months, waiting for the opportunity to strike."

Slamming his hand down on the chair, Tiny stood, kicking the chair away.

Ned stared at the picture. "I didn't even give a thought to him being new at all this. This is my fucking fault. I should never have taken that order."

Tiny gripped the ledge of the window staring into the gym. "He's got my town, and there's not enough time. I've got one of my men keeping the girls safe for now, but I know it's not going to stay that way."

"What do you need from me? This fucker is going down," Ned said.

"Get me to Fort Wills undetected. I don't know what Snitch has in place. Get me through the airport and landed on good soil. Devil is collecting my men. He's given me two days. His men are riding hard. They're not too far away, and he was already on his way to Fort Wills when I called him." Tiny folded his arms.

"Then make that two," Eva said, standing up. "I'm going with him."

"No, you're not going anywhere," Tiny and Ned said together.

"Yeah, I'm going with him." She turned to Tiny.

"We can't find Murphy. Tate is going to need me." Lash and Nash had finally gotten in touch last night while she'd been calling for Murphy. The two brothers were holed up in an apartment ten miles out of Fort Wills. They were injured but healing.

Still, Murphy was missing.

"You know I'm making sense. Tate will not listen to you."

"You're not going into a killing zone," Ned said.

"Dad, I'm not eighteen anymore or a child. I'm going with Tiny. My home is with him." She linked her arm through his. "We can do this together, not alone."

Tiny knew she spoke the truth. Until Murphy was found, Tate was going to be impossible to handle. His daughter was never going to be easy.

"Fine, we go together, but you stay by my side and you're armed. I'm not taking you into a killing zone," Tiny said.

"I'm coming as well," Alex said.

"No." Tiny yelled the word. "Until Murphy is found, dead or alive, you're staying here doing everything you can to locate him. He's my son-in-law, and I'm not losing him."

"I can get you closer to Fort Wills. Everything else will be up to you," Ned said.

"Get me to Fort Wills and we'll be even."

"Good." Ned walked around the desk and offered Tiny his hand. He took it, shaking the hand of the father of the woman he was going to marry.

The fist to the face he wasn't expecting.

"Dad!"

Tiny stumbled back.

"You hurt my girl again, and I'll hand her your head in a body bag," Ned said. Both men had an agreement. Nodding his head, Tiny stood then shook

Ned's hand.

It was time for business and to kill the man intent on destroying him.

****

Two days later

Eva was nervous as she watched Tiny getting dressed. They'd landed at the airport yesterday, and he'd spent the last twenty-four hours preparing to confront Snitch by keeping in touch with Devil and knowing his time frame for arrival. Devil had most of his men and was heading back to Fort Wills right now.

"Don't you think you need to wait this out?" Eva asked.

"No. I don't need to wait this out. Snitch and I have a history. There is no chance I'm letting him get away with hunting my boys and taking them out. Have you called Killer?" Tiny asked.

"He's on his way to pick you up." They were staying in the old warehouse where they'd kept Nash. Eva didn't have a problem staying in the warehouse. What she had a problem with was knowing Tiny was walking to his death.

"You shouldn't go. Wait until Devil with your men show up." She was panicking. What if something happened to Devil, and his men were attacked again?

"Element of surprise. Devil coming in with his club would spoil everything. I've got to take Snitch now." Tiny secured the safety on his gun and placed it in the back of his jeans.

"Or he could shoot you in the head making all of this a waste of time."

"It's not going to happen. Shooting me in the head is not Snitch's style. After what I did to him he's going to take his time over me. He can't have Mikey. He's dead. Snitch will settle for me. Trust me, baby. I've got this." He cupped her face, pressing a kiss to her lips.

"And what if you don't?" she asked, following him outside.

"Look, this man is responsible for killing innocent people. I really don't give a fuck about him right now. I'm working to make this place safe." He took her hands, holding her close. "To make you safe. I know Snitch. He likes to have an audience when shit goes down. It's why he has a new club."

"I'm scared, Tiny. How do you know Devil will pull through? What if he's working with Snitch?" Her hands were shaking as she held onto Tiny's jacket.

"Devil has a score to settle with Snitch, and he helped me get rid of him last time. I trust him. Trust me, Eva. I'm coming home to you, baby."

There was nothing more she could do.

"Do you have the number Alex gave you?" he asked.

She handed him the white slip of paper with Snitch's number on it.

"I'm coming back from this, and then we're going to get married." He caressed her cheek.

All too soon he was pressing the buttons on his cell phone and putting it to his ear. She wanted to snatch the phone off him. Instead, she stood listening to what was happening.

"Who the fuck is this?" She heard the man snarl over the line.

"Hello, Snitch."

Standing close, Eva listened in to the conversation.

"What the fuck?"

"Yeah, you can't fucking kill me, Snitch. It's time you and I settle this once and for all."

Tiny stepped away, and she didn't get to hear

Snitch's reply.

"Gladly. Let's end this." The cell phone was dropped and smashed into the ground.

"You shouldn't do this."

"I'll have Killer with me." The sound of a car approaching had her looking over her shoulder to see the man himself approaching.

"I want you to head on over to Tate and the others. Killer kept them off their scent by killing one of Snitch's men. I want you to keep them calm, and I'll get to you as soon as I'm done," Tiny said, getting into the car.

"What exactly do you want me to say?" she asked, leaning against the car.

"Tell Tate I'm handling it. Play cards, cook, I don't know. Do something that will keep her mind off everything else," Tiny said.

Glancing over at Killer, Eva shot him a glare. "You keep him alive, or you'll answer to me."

"Yes, Boss lady." Killer smiled even though his expression was all serious.

Stepping back, she watched the men drive away. Fear tightened around her heart, but she kept it at bay. Heading back inside the warehouse, he grabbed her backpack and hiked it on her shoulder. She wore a pair of jeans, a long shirt of Tiny's, and a pair of pumps. Eva hadn't given it much thought to walking to town, but she didn't have much choice.

Exiting the warehouse, she headed in the direction of town and turned her own cell phone on. She dialed Tate's number.

"Do you have any news on Murphy?" Tate asked.

Eva sighed. "No, I've not got anything on him, Tate. I'm headed your way. Where are you?"

"We're stuck in Kelsey's apartment. Killer left a

little while ago leaving a gun for our protection." She listened to the younger woman knowing interrupting Tate's flow would make her remember Murphy was missing.

Suddenly Tate stopped. "I can't raise this baby without him, Eva."

"We're all hoping that's not the case." Even as she said the words, Eva felt her hope disappearing.

"He should have phoned by now or gotten in touch. You and I both know it's not good if he's not gotten in touch."

"Stop thinking about it, Tate. That's an order." The sound of bikes approaching made Eva tense. She looked behind her to see the emblem Tiny described. Turning back to face the road, she swallowed past the lump in her throat.

"Shit, is that them?" Tate asked.

"Yes, be calm. Hopefully they'll pass." Eva started laughing and talking about a comedy movie she'd seen a few weeks ago. Tate didn't say anything, which Eva was thankful for.

The bikes slowed down beside her. Eva couldn't believe the rotten fucking luck. "You really should have seen it," Eva said, almost slipping up by saying Tate's name.

"Miss," a man said.

Taking a breath, Eva turned around, trying to look unaffected by the bikes. She recognized the man from the photo she'd seen of Snitch.

"Hold on a minute, honey. I think some guy has stopped to ask me for directions." Dropping the phone, she smiled at Snitch, wishing she could beat the shit out of him and save Tiny the trouble. "Can I help you?"

Snitch stared at her. "Are you from around here?"

"No, I'm just wandering through. Backpacking

my way across the states. My mom and dad are funding it. I'm trying to find myself."

Shut up, you're giving away too much information.

"Can I help you with anything?" she asked.

He kept his gaze on her, looking her up and down.

"Look, mister, I've got to go."

"Where is he?" Snitch asked.

"Who? I don't have a clue who you're talking about," Eva said. *Crap.* Something in the way he was looking at her unnerved her.

"Tiny, where is he?"

Eva frowned, trying to pretend she didn't have the first clue who Tiny was.

"You're Tiny's whore. Don't even try to deny it."

Snitch climbed off his bike. Eva didn't need further warning. She ran in the opposite direction hoping to get away.

She knew her quick getaway wouldn't work, but she tried. Snitch slammed her to the ground.

"Leave me alone," she said, screaming. No one came to her help. She felt the sniggers behind her from his men who were laughing and mocking her attempt to escape.

He grabbed her hair, pulling her head back. "I know Tiny. He's got something planned for me. The one thing I know is he won't let a fucking thing happen to you."

His hand went around her throat, choking her. She cried out, clawing at his hand.

"No wonder he loves you." Snitch caressed a hand down her side. "You're some fucking piece of meat. I can't wait to get my dick wet."

Snitch picked her up off the floor and carried her

back to his men. She struggled against him, dropping her phone and backpack.

"Leave me alone." Eva screamed as he back handed her. Hitting the floor, Eva hoped Tiny would make this bastard pay. There was evil inside him, and if Tiny didn't win, God help them all.

"You either hold on, bitch, or you fall off." Eva held onto Snitch's waist. Falling off was not in her future if she could help it. She wanted to see Tiny end this motherfucker.

Chapter Thirteen

Tiny stood on the outskirts of Fort Wills. Killer had driven off and was coming back with the Chaos Bleeds crew. Devil was not far from the town, and he trusted the other leader to right their past mistake.

The sound of rumbling bikes made him aware of Snitch getting closer. It was time to end the past. Reaching behind his back, he felt the gun he was going to use to end Snitch. He shouldn't be happy or feel joy at the thought of ending another man. Tiny couldn't stop it, though. This day wasn't going to end until he watched Snitch take his last breath.

It's been a long time fucking coming.

The smile on his face dropped when he saw the person on the back of Snitch's bike. Blood was coming from her lip, and anger replaced any satisfaction of killing him. A swift kill was too fucking nice to this piece of shit. Tiny was going to take his time and make him pay for everything he'd done and all the men, women, and children the fucker had hurt.

He watched as the men turned their bikes off and climbed off the machines. These men were responsible for hurting his own men. Tiny knew his men, and they would be after blood.

"So, you do come back from the fucking dead," Snitch said, grabbing Eva by the hair.

"I'm sorry, Tiny. I was going to town, and they passed. I tried to escape," she said. He was shocked to see the anger on her face rather than the fear.

Don't worry, baby. I'll get us both out of this mess.

"Shut it," Snitch said, punching her in the ribs. She went down, grabbing her side. Tiny fisted his hands, wanting to sink his knuckles into the man's face. He was going to pay the bastard back for all the fucked up memories he had.

If Mikey was still alive, the old bastard would be exacting revenge along with him.

"So, Tiny, you're here, surrounded by my men. What the fuck do you think you can do?" Snitch asked.

Staring at the man, Tiny tried to blank out Eva. He needed to be able to think as otherwise he was fucked. "I heard you were one man down."

Snitch reacted, producing a knife, which he put to Eva's throat. "Do I look like I'm in the fucking joking mood? I will slit your slut's throat, and I'll do it for fucking fun. You know I will."

"You're not leaving here alive, Snitch. You should have died long ago."

"Is this what this is about? The slut you saw me fuck? The bitch I fucking killed. I've got news for you. She wasn't the first woman I put in the ground. I've got a whole fucking list of dead bodies to my name. What do you think you can do, Tiny? You've got nothing. I've got your woman, and all my men are ready to put holes in your body," Snitch said.

Eva was struggling against the other man. Tiny was proud of her fight. His woman was never going to give up, not even to a man like Snitch.

Smiling, Tiny stared at his enemy. Memories of the night Snitch had hurt that girl flooded him. If he died today and took Snitch with him, Tiny would be happy. Ending Snitch would make him feel better, and that was all Tiny needed to feel in that moment, better.

"You've got no men. What do you have to smile about?" Snitch asked.

Tiny didn't bother answering the other man. "You've got no idea what's coming to you."

Snitch leaned down, licking Eva's cheek. He

grabbed her breast, squeezing her hard. Eva howled in pain at the hard grip of her tit. Tiny tensed knowing he was going to kill Snitch over and over again. "Your woman has a lot of meat on her, Tiny. I can hurt her a lot, and she won't even break."

Disgust clawed at him. His stomach turned as sickness threatened. Tiny held everything in, refusing to back down as he kept Snitch in his sights. Everything was in place. He had to bide his time otherwise everything would fail.

"Remember what I said to you, baby," Tiny said.

"I know. I remember."

The cell phone he hadn't destroyed buzzed against his leg. It was time to get this show on the road. Snitch had thought he was in control, and all along he didn't have a clue what was about to happen. "Tell me, Snitch, did any of your men find my own men dead on that road?" Tiny asked.

"They fucking died. We saw to that." Snitch yelled, spitting onto the ground. "Over twenty years ago you sent me out of his fucking town, and I had to start again from the beginning. Now it's time for me to take it the fuck back."

Tiny glanced over Snitch's shoulder seeing what he was waiting for. The rumbling of bikes sounded first. Devil was on his way, and Snitch was living his last few moments.

"Snitch, what do we do?" one of his men asked.

"This town is ours. The Skulls are fucking dead, and I'm going to take this bitch as my whore and use her like I used that slut on that night." Tiny tensed as he saw Snitch smirk. "I saw you that night. The disgust on your face at what was happening. I had my gun trained on you the whole time. I thought about taking you out, but then I thought of a better game of making you rape a woman for your life."

Tiny knew none of that had ever happened. He'd gotten away before Snitch could destroy him.

"The slut screamed so fucking good. I wonder if your woman knows how to scream just like I like." One of his hands went between her thighs. Tiny tensed, ready to fuck up his whole plan.

Eva jerked out of Snitch's arms, rounded on him and slapped her palm across his face. "Don't you fucking touch me, you fucking pig." She spat into his face.

Wiping the spittle from his face, Snitch backhanded her, sending her to the ground.

Hold steady. Don't fuck this up. You can cut his balls off and feed them to him all in good time.

A kick landed to her stomach, and Tiny couldn't handle it anymore. Charging at Snitch, he forced the other man to the ground. He'd do everything to keep Eva safe. The sound of the bikes was growing louder. It was only a matter of time before they got there.

Snitch landed a jab to his cheek sending Tiny down to the ground. He wasn't stunned too long before he kicked Snitch in the stomach. They tumbled together, landing blows to the stomach, chest, and face. Tiny ended on top of him with Snitch facing the floor.

"Do you know why you're going to lose this fight, Snitch?" Tiny asked. Snitch struggled but didn't give the order for his men to intervene. He heard Eva gasping in pain. This fucker was going to know torture before he killed him.

"You're a fucking ass." Jerking Snitch's head up at the approaching bikes, Tiny forced him to look.

"You've never been a good leader, Snitch. Your men will desert you faster than a fucking woman who knows the scent of death. My men are fucking loyal to me. They know what I want, and they fight for me. They know I'm the fucking boss."

Standing up, Tiny released Snitch in time to see all of his men climb off the back off the bikes of Chaos Bleeds. Lash and Nash were the first men to approach. They were carrying crowbars by their sides. Tiny saw the anger on the men's faces. They wanted revenge, and it was so close they could probably taste it.

Devil climbed off the bike with Murphy behind him. Tiny tensed when he saw the bandage across half of Murphy's face. He'd not been able to find him. How the fuck had Devil found him? Murphy looked the worse for wear.

"Don't worry, Tiny, I'm still fucking pretty," Murphy said, holding a gun by his side.

Smiling, Tiny was so fucking relieved to see the other man. Now was not the time to ask questions. Snitch kicked him in the leg, sending him down.

Tiny heard the fighting start as he lashed out at Snitch.

Snitch sliced down, catching his arm. Tiny growled, feeling the sting of the blade.

Gunshots went off, but the only sounds he heard were the sounds of Snitch's men, failing. The Skulls were hard and wouldn't let the other biker club get away with it. Also, they had Chaos Bleeds on their side. Devil and his men made a hard impenetrable wall.

Kicking out, Tiny threw Snitch off him. He dove on the other man sending them both to the floor.

Snitch landed a hit to his temple. Tiny's head hit the floor dazing him from the impact. Turning, he saw Snitch with a gun pointed at his temple. This was the end. Tiny didn't want to die. There was so much for him to live for, but he wasn't going to beg this bastard for his life.

Staring down the barrel of the gun, Tiny waited,

determined not to run from death.

****

Murphy was alive. Eva felt a brief glimpse of happiness, which ended quickly as she watched the fighting around her. Every part of her body ached. She never thought she'd be so happy at the sight of all the men, but even bruised, she was happy to see them. Murphy's bandaged face was even a pleasure to see.

Why hadn't she been able to locate him?

Turning around, she froze as she caught sight of Snitch holding a gun pointed directly at Tiny's head.

No, he was not going to die. She would not let her man go so easily. It wasn't happening. Eva screamed, but the sound was drowned out by all the fighting. Out of the corner of her eye she spotted the gun. Reaching out, she flicked the safety off. Her father and Tiny had both taught her how to use a gun. Getting to her feet, she ran the several steps to where Snitch stood over Tiny.

"I'm going to fuck her ten times a fucking day, and every time I'm going to make her remember how I put a bullet in you. She'll be begging for my cock, and when she wants me I'll fucking kill her." Snitch was sneering and gloating. His words made Eva feel sick.

Her stomach turned, but she kept the vomit inside. Raising her gun, she pressed it to Snitch's temple.

"That's my man," Eva said.

"You're not going to shoot me," Snitch said. She saw him tense. Not taking her eyes off her target, Eva tensed, knowing the warm flush running over her was coming from what she was about to do. She'd never killed anyone, and she was about to end a life right now.

He's going to kill you and your man. Kill him. Save Tiny.

"I'm going to shoot you. Your biggest mistake, Snitch, was coming out of hiding."

He turned, but it was too late. She pulled the trigger and ended Snitch's life. The bullet went through his head, tearing out the back. Eva watched the body fall. Tiny kicked it off him before the body collapsed on him.

The fighting had mellowed down. Looking around her, holding the gun in her hand, Eva bent over and vomited everything she'd eaten that day, coating the ground.

Tiny wrapped his arm around her waist, rubbing her back as she hurled everything out.

I've killed a man. I've killed a man.

"I've got you, baby."

She continued to throw up until there was nothing left. Sinking against Tiny, she held on tightly to him, needing the comfort only he could give. "He was going to kill you."

"I know. You saved me, baby. Thank you." He stroked her back and hair. "I'm not going to kiss you until you brush your teeth. Vomit breath is not what I want to remember."

Eva laughed, slapping him on the arm.

"Your woman is fucking hot," Devil said, walking closer. She looked at him over her shoulder. "Will you be giving her away any time soon?"

"Not a chance, and if you try I'll cut your balls off," Tiny said.

Devil put his hands up in the air. "I'm taken, man. Got a bitch of my own who'll be missing me, if she hasn't taken off that is." Devil whistled, rounding up his men. "We'll clean this shit up, and then we'll be on the road."

Tiny offered him the hand that wasn't wrapped tightly around her. "It's a pleasure doing business with you." Devil shook his hand. She saw the smile on his face.

"It's fantastic to have that sick fuck in the ground. I wouldn't miss it for the world." She stayed by Tiny's side while the men cleaned away the bodies. Tiny was talking with all of his men.

She didn't know how long they were stood there until Tiny finally made his way over to her. Killer was sat behind the wheel, tapping his fingers on it.

"Call the women. Tell them to come to my house," Tiny said, leaning into the car. Eva wrapped her arms around his neck, holding him close. "How are you doing, baby?"

"I'm fine." And she was, which bothered her. She'd taken a life and didn't care. Snitch was evil and was about to hurt her man.

"Devil and his boys are going to give us a ride through town. They're going to know The Skulls are back."

"This was your plan all along?" Eva asked.

"Nah, this was Alex's plan. He knows what he's doing."

She smiled, running her hand down his chest. "I couldn't handle anything happening to you."

Cupping her face, Tiny pressed his lips to hers. "You're still not getting tongue."

Slapping him away, she climbed into the car. Tiny moved in the front, and Killer headed out. All the men had worked together to get rid of the evidence. Eva didn't care about the bodies. She imagined the men who stayed behind were going to take care of the final clearance.

The journey to his house was short. Eva held his hand not wanting to let go of the warmth he offered her.

"Everything is going to be okay, baby," Tiny said.

She believed him. The threat hanging over The

Skulls was finally gone. Now was a time for celebration rather than being somber.

Tate rushed toward the car as they pulled into the driveway. Tiny got out, and Eva stepped out behind him. She watched Tate hit her father.

"What the fuck were you thinking? You could have been killed. Where's Murphy? I need to see him," Tate said, sobbing. Angel and Sophia stood by the door with Kelsey, pale. "Where's Eva? Someone took her."

"I'm here, sweety," Eva said, smiling over Tiny's shoulder. In the next breath, Tate had her arms wrapped around Eva, squeezing her.

Within half an hour the sounds of bikes started to get louder. Eva stood next to Tiny as Devil escorted Murphy into the driveway.

Tate's hand went to her stomach as he eased off the bike. "Hey, baby."

"Murphy?"

"Yeah, I know I'm a little fucked up right now, but I still love you. You'll just have to deal with me being a little scarred." Tate rushed forward, grabbing the lapels of his jacket.

"You fucking idiot, Murphy. I love you. I don't give a fuck what you look like. I love you." She went to cup his face but stopped. "I thought the worst."

"It's going to take more than an exploding bike to be rid of me, woman. I'm sticking around, and I've got a baby to help raise."

Eva's heart went out to the young couple. Devil walked to them. "I found him coming out of a hospital about ten miles out that way." He pointed east. "He couldn't remember the number to call Alex. His face is scarred and I think burned. Murphy wanted to come and see his woman."

"Thank you," Tiny said. "I couldn't stand to

come home without him."

"Thank you for putting our past in the ground. Me and my boys are out of here." Devil waved, leaving them alone.

Staying in Tiny's arms, she watched Nash and Lash run to their women. They wrapped their arms around their women. Angel crumbled against Lash. She saw Lash whisper against her ear, stroking her back.

"I've got you, Angel. I'm never leaving you. You're the reason I made it back."

"Don't leave me," Angel said.

Angel and Lash's reunion was sweet and tender. Sophia jumped up against Nash, wrapped her legs around his waist, and refused to let go.

"Before you all leave I just want to say that we'll be bringing the bodies back of Gunn and Time. We'll have a burial and honor their memory along with all of those who have fallen," Tiny said.

All of his men were somber at the news of their two fallen men. A few minutes of silence passed before they started moving.

The men walked into the house, and Tiny took her hand, leading her away to the Fort Wills cemetery.

"The boys will be waiting for us," Eva said, wiping her mouth and finding blood.

"Stink has gone to get Sandy. She'll be patching us up, and Tate will take care of everyone. She needs to keep busy, or she'll freak out on us." Tiny walked around three rows of grave stones before he stopped in front of a modest angel. There were no markings besides the words, "left this life too soon".

"What's this?" Eva asked.

"This is the girl who saved my life," Tiny said. "If I hadn't seen what those fucking animals were doing I would have ended up like them."

Turning to him, Eva wound her hands around his neck. "You becoming like Snitch and the rest of them is not possible. You're too good to let something like that happen."

"It's not true. I was falling in that path."

"You're good, Tiny. In here where it counts, you're good," she said, pressing her palm against his chest. "I love you so much, and I know you wouldn't let anything happen to me or your men."

She had faith in him where everything else had failed.

"I was pleased to see him dead, Eva."

"I was pleased to kill him." She tapped his chest. "His blood is on my hands."

"I wish I could take that away from you."

Eva gave him a sad smile. "There's nothing we can do about that. We're together, and with time we'll be strong."

"You're sticking around?" he asked, smiling.

"Yeah, I'm sticking around."

They made their way to the compound, which was just a pile of ash. She felt Tiny sigh against her.

"You'll rebuild. It'll take time, and before you know it, you'll be back to doing your runs, sweet-butts getting naked—"

"And the bikers finding their women?" he asked.

"Yeah."

Tiny stroked her waist, pulling her in close. "So, Evangeline Walker, what do you want for your perfect wedding?"

Giggling, Eva shook her head. "You're not ready for that answer." She rubbed her nose against his. "I can give you a clue. None of you are wearing leather."

He groaned, and she silenced him with her lips.

Chapter Fourteen

Apart from Murphy, none of The Skulls ended up in the hospital. Tiny made sure Murphy had the best care. He would have the scars and the memories of what happened, which Tiny wished he could erase. What Snitch did to all of them wouldn't be soon forgotten, and neither would Time or Gunn. Stink brought Sandy back, and the woman looked happy to be putting all of them back together. Tiny wondered if she regretted quitting work. If she did then he'd find some way to get her the old job back. Sandy was a lovely woman, talented, and she didn't deserve to lose any of it. After he was patched up, Zero disappeared for a week. No one knew where he went and Tiny didn't mind as long as he was safe. Since the ambush, Tiny figured they all deserved a fun break away from the club.

Tiny's biggest fear was Eva and the plans she had for the wedding. What scared him more was the fact his daughter was getting involved. In fact, Tate was arranging everything. He wasn't getting married in his club, but a week after the confrontation with Snitch they started the rebuild of the compound. The workers in Fort Wills were more than happy to work on the new club for The Skulls.

The two men who lost their lives were remembered, along with Gunn and Time, and Tiny arranged, paid for, and attended the funerals of the men who were lost. All of The Skulls were present, and the memorial lasted into the night with alcohol and food flowing. Throughout it all, Tiny had his rock, Eva. She was more than he could have ever asked for.

She brightened his world even though she carried a wedding magazine around with her all the time. The fear wasn't of the magazine but of his daughter.

He kept in touch with Devil. The other man was a hard nut but had come through for Tiny and the boys when it was needed. No matter if their scores were settled, Tiny felt indebted to him and Chaos Bleeds. Tiny knew that without them, he wouldn't have his men back or his town.

Ned gave his blessing, and Gavin had no choice but to move on after Tiny kicked his ass in a one off visit to Vegas. Alex moved back to Fort Wills. The Vegas lifestyle had lost its edge. Tiny was happy for the company, and Alex got his own leather cut. Admittedly, Alex preferred his business suits to the leather.

Three months later Tiny stood in front of a mirror glaring at the bow tie wrapped around his neck choking the life out of him.

"Dude, I thought my woman was bad," Lash said, walking into the room to slap him on the back.

Tate was the matron of honor while Sophia, Kelsey, and Angel were bridesmaids along with Sandy. The other woman had stuck around and lived with Stink in a platonic friendship. Tiny knew Stink wished it was different. He couldn't force women to give his men a chance even though he wished it was the case. Killer was moping around because Kelsey only wanted to be friends.

Killer was a good man and had protected his women when Tiny couldn't.

"Shut the fuck up. This is what Eva wanted," Tiny said, tugging on the tie around his neck. He felt trapped with the tight clothing. Thinking about Eva and the happiness he'd see made him stop tugging.

"I thought Tate was insane with her baby shower and wedding, but this is too much," Murphy said. One side of his face was still bandaged after his latest hospital appointment.

"I'll never forget all that fucking pink," Nash said, shuddering.

Angel, Sophia, and Tate were all starting to show. Tiny was nervous to be a granddaddy. He didn't feel old enough to be a granddaddy.

Shaking his head, he stared at his men feeling proud of what he'd created.

Eva demanded a church wedding where all of his men wore proper suits with top hats and kept their language to a minimum. This was the dream wedding she'd imagined as a child. Ned had flown in to give her away.

"We've got to go. I can't stick around here waiting. I need to get there and hope she comes to me at the altar." Last night he'd dreamed she left him stood there, waiting for her to collect him. Checking his cuffs, he headed outside to hear the guests talking. Walking down the aisle he stood in front of the priest. He didn't look behind him, but he knew the two areas were separated. On one side were his men and some of the townsfolk while on the other Eva's father and his boys who were her family also stood waiting for the event.

Ned had given him a warning about hurting Eva, but Tiny wouldn't be hurting the woman he loved.

"Sir, are you ready?" the priest asked.

"We will be." He nodded at the priest and gave him a smile. Tiny had never been married in a church like this with rose petals dotting the aisle. He'd married Patricia in a cheap church in Vegas.

Silence fell on the room, and the music started up.

"Tiny, you're up," Alex said, standing beside his side. Alex was his best man and held the ring he intended to use to claim his woman.

Turning toward his woman, Tiny felt desire lurch inside him replacing anything else he was thinking. Eva looked up at him and smiled. She wore a beautiful white gown that cupped her breasts showing a generous curve of cleavage. The dress had no arms or shoulders, and instead it billowed out making her look like a princess. The veil she wore was down her back, her face exposed for him to see.

The moment he looked at her, everything else fell away. This was what he wanted and who he wanted to spend the rest of his life with.

Ned cleared his throat, and Tiny thanked him, taking Eva from her father. "I'll take care of her."

"You better."

Tiny was sure Ned threatened to kill him as he walked away. He didn't care. Eva was by his side, ready to become his wife. Facing his woman, Tiny listened to the priest and said his words.

Soon he was sliding his ring onto her finger, and Eva turned to Tate. His daughter moved forward. Her stomach was nicely rounded showing her budding motherhood.

Eva slid a ring on his finger, and the priest said those special words. They were drowned out as he claimed her lips and the crowd erupted in whistles, cheers, and applause.

"You're mine now, Eva. You can't run from me."

"I can run. It just means when you catch me we can have a lot more fun."

Sinking his hand into her hair, he tilted her head back to slam his lips back on hers. There was nowhere else he wanted to be other than in her arms feeling her lips on his. "I love you," he said.

"It's time for photos," Tate said, squealing.

The rest of the day went by in a blur as Tiny kept Eva by his side. The only time he released her was when she danced with her father. He watched her never taking his eyes off her.

Sipping at his wine, Tiny knew nothing else could go wrong. His love for Eva would get him through.
****

Seven months later

Eva groaned as Tiny rubbed lotion into her skin. They'd been married for seven months, and they'd only just got around to going on their honeymoon. She didn't want to leave the club as they were dealing with the compound rebuild. Tate had given birth to a beautiful bouncing boy. Eva remembered the screaming as Tate hadn't made it to the hospital. She'd given birth at home. Angel did better, giving birth to a son, but she'd made it to hospital. Lash stayed with her in the room, holding her hand as his son was brought into the world. Sophia was last giving Nash a daughter. Eva chuckled thinking about the look on Nash's face when he realized he'd be raising a girl and looking at Tate. The man had looked petrified. The last few months had been magical even if she was now a grandma at the ripe old age of twenty-nine. She didn't mind at all.

With everything happening she hadn't given any thought to finding the time for a honeymoon. Only when his men had sent them to the airport with their honeymoon booked did Eva think it best to leave.

"Are you ready for me to fuck you again?" Tiny asked, rubbing lotion against her legs. Alex had given them three weeks at his private villa on his private island. Eva didn't know where as they'd not been disturbed by anyone. Also, she was lying on the beach naked as a very naked Tiny was massaging oil into her skin.

Her body was on fire for him.

Tiny turned her over and began to suck on her nipples. "So fucking big and full." He kissed one breast and then the next.

His hands dropped down to the curve of her stomach. They stared at each other, and Eva smiled. "Are you feeling a bit possessive, Daddy?" she asked, leaning up to kiss his cheek.

She'd found the news out a month ago. Eva was pregnant with his baby. Tiny had looked pale when she told him the news. He'd then announced a party and celebration with the fact he was going to be a father again.

Tate loved the news. She'd always wanted a younger brother or sister to boss around.

"What do you think it is?" Tiny asked, touching her stomach.

"I don't know. Do you care?"

"No, not really. Well, yes, if it's a girl I think we've had enough from Tate to last us a long time. A boy is even worse. Look at Nash and Lash," Tiny said.

Her arousal didn't diminish. Leaning up, she cupped his cheek and kissed his lips. "Tate is a woman to be proud of. She's got a Skull who loves her and a beautiful son. Lash and Nash are both brilliant fathers. They're good boys, and we're going to have a son or daughter who'll make you proud." She covered his hand over her stomach. "Now shut up and fuck me."

Tiny gave her everything she needed and more. Seven months later, Tiny got more than he bargained for as Eva gave birth to twins, a boy and a girl.

Epilogue

Killer stood beside his bike waiting for Kelsey to get out of work. For the last year they'd rarely seen each other between the successful rebuild of the compound, and with him going between Vegas and Fort Wills, Killer hadn't the time to visit her. He'd seen Kelsey when she visited Tate at the club house. Beside the few glances, he never got the chance to see her. He'd been the one nominated to go with Alex whenever the need arose.

Tiny wouldn't leave his wife and twins, and none of the other boys wanted to go to Vegas.

He was back, the compound was finished, and he was able to show Kelsey he was ready for a commitment. After Snitch he'd avoided her looking at him. She knew he was the one responsible for killing one of their men. He didn't know if the knowledge affected her, but he wasn't prepared to take that risk.

Women left the dental surgery, giggling as they saw him. He didn't give them any of his attention. Kelsey walked out, looking toward him. Her hair was longer, and she'd allowed the cherry blonde color to seep out to the light brown of her normal hair color.

"Killer," she said, smiling.

Her approach was awkward. All he wanted to do was draw her into his arms. Killer hadn't felt the pleasure of another woman in such a long time.

"Hey, Kels. How are you?" he asked.

"I'm doing good. You're back in Fort Wills?"

"Yeah." He reached out, taking her hand.

She didn't pull away from his touch as she looked him up and down. "I haven't seen you around. I didn't get chance to ask Tate how you were doing."

"I've been back and to and from Vegas. Club shit needed sorting out." Standing up, he offered to walk with her. "Kels, there is something I want to talk to you about," he said, walking beside her.

"Really? What about?" She pulled her hand away as they walked toward her building. He liked the fact they were not too far from where she lived.

"I was hoping that you would go out with me." His palms were all sweaty as he stared at her.

Kelsey looked hopeful, and then her face dropped as she looked behind him. While he'd been thinking about the best way to ask her on a date a limo had driven up behind him.

"What's the matter?" he asked, taking hold of her hand. The driver climbed out, moved to the back, and opened the door.

A man in a tailored suit climbed out. Killer looked him up and down as he approached Kelsey.

His woman's hands were all sweaty.

"You promised you wouldn't come here," Kelsey said, talking to the man.

"You wouldn't answer my calls, and I've finally gotten some free time." The man looked at where Killer was holding her hand. "Am I interrupting something?"

"Yeah, you are. Who the fuck are you?" Killer asked.

"Killer, I think it's best you leave. I've give you a call." Kelsey tried to push him away, but he wasn't moving. He wanted to know what was going on with this fucking prick stood right in front of him.

"I'm Michael Granito, Kelsey's husband."

The End

TINY

EVERNIGHT PUBLISHING ®

www.evernightpublishing.com

CPSIA information can be obtained
at www.ICGtesting.com
Printed in the USA
LVHW040055190419
614781LV00001B/20